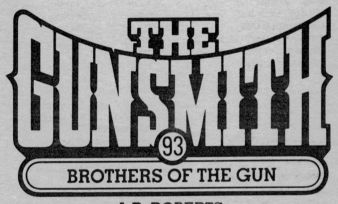

THE GUNSMITH

93

BROTHERS OF THE GUN

J. R. ROBERTS

JOVE BOOKS, NEW YORK

THE GUNSMITH #93: BROTHERS OF THE GUN

A Jove Book / published by arrangement with
the author

PRINTING HISTORY
Jove edition / September 1989

ISBN: 0-515-10132-X

Jove Books are published by The Berkley Publishing Group,
200 Madison Avenue, New York, New York 10016.
The name "JOVE" and the "J" logo
are trademarks belonging to Jove Publications, Inc.

PRINTED IN THE UNITED STATES OF AMERICA

10 9 8 7 6 5 4 3 2 1

ONE

The Gunsmith was in a fine mood as he rode out of Carson City, Nevada, and headed up Gold Canyon on his way to the Comstock Lode. The air was cool and the sky was cloudless. Duke, his handsome black gelding, was feeling frisky and had been curried until he shone, and it was clear the animal was eager to be on the trail again after spending a few leisurely days in Carson City. Nevada's capital lay at the base of the eastern slope of the Sierra Nevadas, and it was one of Clint's favorite places. The high desert country was healthful and the thin air was invigorating to both man and animal. If a fella got too warm in the summer, he could ride up into the Ponderosa Pines that ringed the great Tahoe basin. And if he wanted good fishing, the Sierra Lakes and the Walker, the Carson and the Truckee that tumbled gaily down the eastern Sierra slopes were all top fishing spots.

But there was no fishing on the Comstock—unless you called hard-rock mining a way of fishing for gold. Clint had not visited the Comstock in many years but he had heard it was booming. Actually, he wasn't headed for Virginia City but, instead, to its smaller sister city, Gold Hill. Silver City, Gold Hill and then Virginia City followed one after the other. Of course, Virginia City was the Queen of the Com-

1

stock, but Gold Hill was a close rival, at least according to what the folks in this part of the country had to say. Each city sort of overflowed into the next because the great Comstock Lode itself was buried deep beneath them all.

Clint had been in the mines of the Comstock and also a few in Colorado and Montana, but it was not an experience he relished. The cold, dank rock and the creaking timbers that supported unimaginably heavy weights gave him an uneasy feeling in the pit of his stomach. A lot of men died in underground mines. Most were the victims of cave-ins, but on the Comstock, a man also had to worry about poisonous gases and huge pockets of hot water that an unwary miner could open and which would either scald him to death or else drown him.

The mighty Comstock Lode was world famous, but few of the miners who came for the high wages ever made much money. Rather, it was the stock speculators and the businessmen who reaped fortunes. And from what Clint had heard, his best childhood friend, Rick Hadley, was one of the men who was on his way to becoming rich.

Clint pulled a creased letter from his pocket and unfolded it after he looped his reins over the saddle horn allowing Duke to simply plod along. The Gunsmith had been working as a range detective up near Cheyenne when the letter had reached him, and Clint still had no idea how his old friend had learned of his whereabouts after almost fifteen years. But Rick had learned of it and had invited the Gunsmith to join him in Gold Hill.

Clint reread aloud the last two lines of the crumpled letter and the words caused him to smile. ''I own the biggest saloon and gambling den in Gold Hill and also a brewery, a hotel and a whorehouse. I figure if a man has a good roof over his head, free whores, cards and all the beer he'll ever want, what else is worth living for? Come see me and you can have as much as you want of everything! Signed, Rick Hadley, (Your old Blood Brother).''

Blood brothers. Clint remembered when they were kids, probably no more than thirteen, they had scratched each other's wrists with a penknife and when their blood flowed, they'd bound their wrists together with a strip of leather. The way Indians were said to do.

The memory caused the Gunsmith to chuckle. He had fought and traveled all over the West as both a lawman and gunsmith, and he'd seen plenty of Indians. Plains Indians like the Cheyenne, Sioux and the Comanche. Coastal Indians like the Cumash as well as the fierce southwestern desert tribes such as the Paiute and the Apache. But he'd never heard of any Indians cutting their wrists and binding them together and then proclaiming themselves to be blood brothers. So the idea was probably nothing more than a dime novel fabrication, but even so, Clint could remember how dead serious the act of mingling blood had seemed to him and Rick Hadley. Apparently, Rick felt the same way because he'd sure mentioned the solemn experience.

As the Gunsmith rode up the canyon, he was amazed at the changes he saw since the last time he had been up this steep, winding grade. For one thing, all the trees had been logged off the slopes. Big trees had never grown in these mountains, only the runty pinion and juniper pines. They had never seemed big enough to use for underground timbering, but someone had sure used them for something because they were gone. Probably burnt for firewood.

For another thing, Clint was surprised at the wagon

traffic that he encountered both coming and going up Gold Canyon. There were huge ore wagons with sides fifteen feet tall, and they were so heavy that as they negotiated the steep downward grade the sound of their screeching wood brakes against iron-rimmed tires could be heard for miles. Freighting tons of ore down to the Carson River for smelting and stamping was a risky business. Returning was much easier on both the drivers and their mules, and Clint also had to weave his way through clots of traffic composed of small buckboards, miners on foot and horseback as well as dozens of Chinese who peddled everything from liniment to cooking oil, fresh fish and plucked ducks. And finally, there were a scattering of Paiute Indians. Shambling, downtrodden people for the most part who had once owned all this land and had been overwhelmed by the white onslaught after the first gold and silver discoveries. Now, the Paiute seemed to consist mostly on selling pathetic little bundles of firewood that they collected on the desert floor or down along the Carson River.

"Hey there!" a freighter yelled, driving his ore wagon straight at Clint and his horse. "I'll run you over for crissakes if you keep gawking like that!"

Clint glanced up at a face full of wild red whiskers surrounding a pair of bloodshot little eyes. "You keep to your side of the road, I'll keep to mine," he yelled.

In answer, the freighter lashed out with his bull-whip and it caught Duke on the muzzle. The black gelding spun away in pain and almost tumbled off the side of the road into a ravine as the big freight wagon rolled past.

Clint dismounted and inspected his horse. A bull-whip or black snake could pluck a man or an animal's eyes out like it was a ripe grape. Duke was missing a big patch of his white blaze, and there was blood where the popper had torn away flesh and hair. "If you're game to teach that man a lesson, I guess I am too," he said between clenched teeth.

Duke seemed to nod his head, and Clint swung back into the saddle and galloped after the wagon and its unsuspecting driver. Clint hopped out of the saddle and trotted along behind the wagon as he tied Duke to its tailgate and then he climbed up the side of the wagon and dropped onto the dusty pile of unprocessed ore.

The screech of brakes was so loud that Clint could have shouted directly into the driver's ear and not have distracted him. Clint chose a better way of making his statement. He drew his six-gun and eased it under the man's slouch hat, stuck the barrel into his wild growth of red whiskers and pulled the trigger.

The gunshot exploded right next to the man's ear and the muzzle blast was enough to catch his beard on fire.

"Holy shit!" the driver screamed, jumping to his feet and slapping at his smoking beard as his lines fell from his hands. "Holy shit!"

Clint stepped back on the mound of ore and grinned with satisfaction. He could not have asked for a more animated and satisfactory reaction as the driver tried to keep his face from becoming a hairy torch.

The driver tore off his hat and jammed it over his beard and that was what finally saved him. He stood balanced before his seat, his mules no longer under his control and his wagon slowly picking up speed.

"Better grab that brake or things are going to get out of control in a hell of a hurry," Clint shouted, pointing at the brake.

The freighter was a huge, round-shouldered brute who probably outweighed the Gunsmith by at least sixty pounds and all of it would be muscle. And it was clear that the man, with his hat clamped over his devastated whiskers and smoking face, wanted nothing more than to attack. But Clint's common sense suggestion could not be ignored. Already, the poor mules were being shoved by the enormous weight of the ore into a trot and soon, they would be in a hopeless race to stay out from under the monstrous wagon chasing them faster and faster down this mountainside.

"I'll get you, you son of a bitch!" the freighter bellowed as he jumped for the brake handle. "I'll kill you!"

Clint looked at what was left of the freighters smoking whiskers and laughed outright. "I'll be in Gold Hill," he yelled as he climbed down from the wagon, untied Duke and jumped into his saddle.

He slowed his horse and watched the ore wagon as it careened around a corner. He could hear the big red-bearded man shouting for everyone to get out of the way of his wagon though he could scarcely be heard over the sound of his screeching brakes.

Clint shook his head. If the freighter was good and real lucky, and if his brake shoe did not burn up before he reached the base of the canyon, then he'd be fine. But if not . . . well, the man was way too free with his black snake, and no one had a right to strike a good horse like Duke. The freighter, like many of his kind, rode fifteen feet above the ground and that made him believe he was better than the rest of mankind.

Clint had seen his type dozens of times and he had little use for them. So now and then, they just had to be taken down a peg or two.

"I'd feel bad if the mules got run over though," he admitted with a shake of his head. "For their sakes, I hope he gets that wagon under control before the next sharp bend in the road sends everything flying.''

Duke nodded his head. A man on foot who had watched the entire affair from the side brush shook his head and drawled, "Mister, when someone rubs your fur the wrong way, you sure don't fuck around with 'em much.''

"I'd have been a little easier on him if he'd have popped me instead of my horse.''

The onlooker was a tired-looking miner dressed in raggedy clothes. "His name is Clyde Blocker and he'll break you in half if he ever gets his hands on you.''

"Thanks for the warning. But the next time I see him, I might put a bullet *through* his ears instead of next to 'em.''

The man's eyes widened. "I'll tell him that. There's plenty of men who have to travel up and down this canyon who'd like nothing better than to see Clyde get his due. I reckon when I tell the story of what I saw just now, he'll be the laughing stock of this canyon.''

Clint just shrugged his shoulders. "Just as long as he stays clear of me, things will be fine. But if he comes looking for trouble, he'll find more than he can handle.''

"You're a gunfighter, that it?''

Clint shook his head. "Not anymore. Now, I'm a gunsmith. A peaceful man simply looking to travel the great highway of life with as little grief as is possible. No different than anyone else.''

"No offense, Mister. But you *are* different than most anyone else I've seen. I don't know of any man who would have dared to do what you did to Clyde.''

Clint saw no point in discussing the matter any

further. During the many years he had spent as a lawman, he'd fought and survived dozens of men like Clyde and some that were a whole lot more dangerous. The Clyde Blockers of the world were bullies. They were big and strong and loved to beat the hell out of smaller, weaker men. But they were vulnerable to a gun and a well placed bullet. Mr. Colt always cut them right down to average size. It was the gunfighters, the hired killers and bushwhackers that were really dangerous, and the most deadly of them all were the most anonymous looking. They didn't wear fancy tied-down holsters and they didn't swagger or bluster. They were quiet and unassuming, but when it was time to do business, they just killed you dead.

"What's your name?" the man called as the Gunsmith continued up the canyon.

"It's Clint Adams!" he yelled.

"You're the Gunsmith! Ain't you!"

"Damn," Clint whispered. "So much for my own anonymity."

TWO

Clint was amazed at how fast Gold Hill had grown since he'd last crossed over the divide that separated it from its big sister, Virginia City. There were storefronts lined solid along both sides of the main street, and the boardwalks were packed with miners blowing off steam while spending their wages. Clint saw an organ grinder with a monkey gathering coins, and a fat lady was dancing to the strum of a banjo as men laughed and drank whiskey straight from the bottle. He passed an alley and saw the dim silhouette of a man vigorously copulating with a whore and just off to the west, a noisy gathering was betting on a cock fight.

As he passed Rick's Brewery, the Gunsmith smiled and took a deep breath of the yeasty smell that never varied from one brewery to another, no matter how good or how bad the beer or ale they made.

"Hey handsome!" a voice called down to him from the upstairs balcony of a hotel room.

Clint looked up to see a buxom blonde leaning on a railing and smoking a Mexican cigarillo. The woman smiled and she had bad teeth, but her dress was so low cut that few men would even notice. Beside her, a slender girl with large blue eyes studied him with interest.

The blonde winked seductively and called out,

"Come on up and play cowboy with me. You be the cowboy, I'll be the horse, and we'll go for a wild ride!"

"Maybe another time," Clint said, looking at the slender woman with the big eyes and shapely legs.

"I ain't gonna save any of it for you!" the blonde yelled loud enough for the entire street to hear. "I got men lined up outside my door day and night!"

Clint laughed and rode on until he came to the biggest saloon in town and sure enough, it had a sign proclaiming it to be RICK'S SALOON.

The Gunsmith tied his horse at the hitching rail and as he unloosened his cinch he glanced over his shoulder through the bat-wing doors. "Sure is a handsome establishment," he said to Duke. "I guess Rick wasn't just gildin' the lilly when he said he was doing right well."

When the cinch was loosened and the Gunsmith was certain that Duke would be fine long enough for him to hunt Rick up and have a few beers, he climbed up on the boardwalk and pushed his way through a noisy crowd toward a polished mahogany bar that was at least a hundred feet long. On his way toward the bar he listened to a woman sing a mournful ballad about a poor Comstock miner who fell down a mine shaft without ever having the chance to tell his lady that he loved her. It was a dumb song with idiotic lyrics but you could have heard a pin drop in the saloon. Grown men were misty-eyed and when the tearful ballad was finally over, the room exploded with an applause thunderous enough to shake the overhead chandeliers.

Even Clint clapped enthusiastically because the singer was a real beauty. She had hair as golden as maple syrup, and a figure that any Greek goddess would have envied.

"Damn!" a man standing next to Clint said in a hoarse throat. "Ain't Miss Honey something though!"

"She sure is," the Gunsmith admitted. "She really knows how to pull a man's heartstrings."

"She could pull on my heartstrings or my draw string," the man said, recovering enough to cackle at his own lewd little joke.

Clint nodded and moved on through the crowd which kept clapping and stomping their feet while shouting for an encore. Clint watched as three beefy men that were obviously saloon bouncers escorted the singer across the room to a back table staked off by a red velvet rope. He saw one of the guards unhook the rope and the other two ushered Miss Honey inside and then fastened the hook again after which all three bouncers folded their muscular arms across their chests and defied anyone to pass.

The crowd, as rough as it was, did not challenge the rope or the bouncers. Clint shook his head and then he nudged a man standing next to him. "What's that rope business?"

"That separates the crowd from going too close to Mr. Rick Hadley's private table," came the answer. "He likes to sit and not be bothered by the rest of us poor, stinking working men."

Clint frowned. "I never heard of such a thing."

"Well, it's the truth. The bastard is too damn good for us anymore. Oh, he sure takes our money, but you can't even rub elbows with him."

"Then how come you're drinking here instead of somewhere else?" Clint asked. "Riding into town, I must have passed at least seven or eight other saloons."

"Sure, there's plenty of saloons but there's only one Miss Honey," came the quick answer. "There ain't no other angels that can sing like her on the

Comstock. Besides, Mr. Hadley, he's always buying the house a round of free beer. His own beer and it's the best in Nevada.''

"So," Clint said with a wry smile. "You don't like the man but you figure you'll let that go by the boards for a song and a free glass of suds.''

"Damn right," the miner said, smacking his lips and emptying his mug. "Damn good beer.''

As if to prove his statement, he belched in Clint's face and then staggered toward the bar to order another glass.

Clint never ceased to be amazed at how cheaply some men would sell out on their convictions. Here was a man spending his money and making another man he did not like wealthy, and all because of a song and an occasional glass of free beer.

Clint pushed his way through the crowd. He had been among rough, working men all his life but these were the smelliest he'd ever been in close contact with. He reminded himself that water was scarcer than gold on the Comstock Lode. Most all of it had to be freighted up in barrels and probably cost almost as much as Rick's beer.

When Clint finally managed to squeeze his way through the crowd to reach the bouncers guarding the velvet rope, he announced, "I'm Rick's friend. I want to see him.''

"Who are you?''

"Clint Adams.''

"Come back later. The boss is busy.''

Clint craned his neck to see over the shoulder of the huge bouncer, but the man was too tall and Rick's table was set far back into the corner where the light was bad. All he could see was the glow of a cigar.

Clint stepped back and addressed all three of the

bouncers. "I have a letter from Rick in my shirt pocket. I'm going to take it out and read it to you and then you had better do what I ask or I'm going to get real impatient."

The middle bouncer had a lantern jaw and shoulders so muscular they looked as if they belonged in a harness. "Let's see the letter," he demanded.

Clint pulled the letter out of his pocket but before he could unfold it, the man snatched it from his hands. That made Clint mad. He stepped back and then he drove his knee up between the bouncer's legs. The bouncer's mouth flew open and he doubled up like a bent nail.

Before the other two could react, Clint's gun was coming up in his fist and he said, "Be foolish and you're gonna get hurt."

The two healthy bouncers froze. Slowly, they lifted their hands and Clint smiled at the one on his right. "You, go tell Rick that his 'blood brother' is here."

"His what?"

"Blood brother. He'll understand."

The man nodded dumbly and turned on his heel very gracefully for one so large. The other that was holding his crushed balls could not straighten yet, but he was half mad with fury. "I'll get you for this."

Clint waited with his gun balanced lightly in the palm of his hand. "That seems to be what everyone on the Comstock is saying these days," he replied in a mild voice. "Freighter told me the very same thing less than thirty minutes ago. I guess I ought to carry a paper and pencil and start a waiting list of big, dumb son of a bitches like you that are intent on rearranging my features."

"Clint? Clint Adams!"

Clint looked up and saw Rick. Rick with that

same wide grin and those magnificent shoulders that had always driven women into fits. Rick with his cleft jaw and dimples, his wavy black hair and perfect teeth. Same Rick only heavier and just a little jowly now.

"Damn," Clint said. "It sure is good to see you, old buddy! I can't tell you how much it pleases me to finally have a rich friend to sponge offa for awhile."

In answer, Rick barked a laugh and pulled up his coat and shirtsleeve. Clint understood and did the same. Even though the light was poor, they could both see the faint wrist scars.

"Blood brothers are forever," Rick said.

"Damn right," Clint answered. "Now, when do I get a taste of your beer and a look at your woman?"

Rick chuckled then ordered them a pitcher of his beer. "Bring the special stuff. You know which that is."

"Yes sir, Mr. Hadley," one of the bouncers said as he hurried off.

Before Clint could ask what the 'special stuff' was, he was being dragged over the velvet rope and back into the dim recesses of what was now obviously a private little alcove with plush red velvet seats and a curtain that could be drawn across the front for privacy.

"Is this your office, or what?" Clint asked.

"You called that right," the saloon owner said. "I like to keep my eye on my own business. You can't do that from behind wooden doors."

It made sense but before Clint could say so, he was presented to the singer who had sung the tear-jerking ballad. In the dim light of candles, she was even more lovely and alluring than she had been on stage.

"Clint Adams," Rick said. "I want you to meet Miss Honey Day."

She stuck out her hand and he took it. "I liked your song," he said.

"Everyone does," she replied, batting her eyelashes.

Clint's smile slipped a little. "I'm sure they do," he said, deciding right on the spot that the last thing this woman seemed to need was another compliment.

"Clint, you old son of a bitch!" Rick shouted. "I was wondering if you got my letter and if you'd ever come visit."

"How can a man resist an offer of a free room, free beer, card games and . . . what was that last thing you mentioned?"

Rick laughed heartily. "You know damn good and well I said I owned a whorehouse and you could have all of that good stuff that you could handle."

"Oh yeah," Clint said, pretending to remember all at once. "Now it comes back to me."

Rick clapped him on the back and gave him another bear hug. "You know," he said, "it's great to be back together again. I've done mighty well and I've met a lot of men since we last saw each other, but I never had a friend like you. Never. I'd like you to think about staying."

Clint had itchy feet and never could stay in any one place more than a month or so, but it wasn't every day that he had offers like the one that Rick had extended. "We'll just wait and see how long you can stand me before we make any commitments," he said.

"Fair enough. I heard it said that you are the fastest gun on this planet."

"Bullshit," Clint said easily.

"Are you still a marshal?"

"Nope."

"Then what?"

Clint shrugged. "I do a little gunsmithin' work. I play cards and even win sometimes. I have a few dollars invested here and there and I'm always finding ways to pick up a few dollars when I get low."

"You stick close to me," Rick said, "and I'll teach you how to make more money than you ever dreamed possible. Isn't that right, Honey?"

"Yeah," she said, reaching out to stroke his thigh in a way that was almost catlike. "You are a real money makin' machine."

Rick liked that description. "I mean to be the biggest saloon owner on the Comstock. I'm planning to open another Rick's Saloon up in Virginia City next week. It'll be the biggest and finest saloon on the lode. You wait and see Clint. I'll find a place for you so that you can make yourself rich, too."

"I'm not interested in being rich," Clint said. "All I want is a few dollars to spend on the things that make life worthwhile. Any more than that is just extra baggage as I travel down the road of life."

"That's nothing but smoke and you know it," Rick said. "Too much whiskey will rot your brains, but a man can never have too much money or sex. Ain't that right!"

Clint glanced at Miss Honey who was watching his face. "Yeah," he said, looking down the front of her dress. "I guess that's the honest truth, Rick. How long do you figure this hot streak of yours is going to last?"

"What do you mean?"

"I mean that all strikes end sooner or later. When they do, everyone picks up and leaves, and the guy that's heavily invested in land or buildings is caught in a tight squeeze."

"Hell, Clint! This Comstock Lode is so big that they'll never find where it ends."

Clint didn't believe a word of that. "How long?" he asked again.

"As long as lady luck and the gold holds out on the Comstock," Rick said. "But even if I'm wrong, I'm still okay. Got a couple of fat bank accounts in San Francisco and I'm always grubstaking a few good prospectors who will strike another payload sooner or later. Until then, I say enjoy life and stop the worrying."

"Sounds good," Clint said, as a bartender came bustling up with a serving tray loaded with cool beer in a brass pitcher.

Rick poured himself and Clint two tall glasses. "To old friends," he said.

Their glasses clinked and Clint added, "And to blood brothers for as long as we live."

They drank then, and the beer was sweet and cool. It was as good a brew as Clint had ever tasted anywhere.

"You really brew this?"

"Naw! I import the good stuff, but what my customers are drinking comes from my own brewery and it ain't far behind. Want to know my secret?"

"Sure."

Rick leaned close. "I use the water from Lake Tahoe. It's the best water in America. The other breweries in Nevada use river water. Hell, that's brackish and worse than piss! But don't tell anybody."

"Not a chance," Clint promised solemnly.

Rick raised his glass in salute, and then he emptied it and poured himself another. "I could use a bodyguard," he said, almost absently.

Clint's smile slipped a little. "I thought that's

what those three gorillas standing in front of the velvet rope were supposed to be.''

''Well, they are,'' Rick said. ''But I'd like a man who could use a gun real well. Better than any man my enemies could hire.''

Clint finished his beer. ''My gun isn't for hire. I'm living the life of a peaceful gunsmith now.''

Rick's face hardened around the corners of his eyes. ''I'm not asking you to fight or shoot anybody. But an important fella like me that is on the rise is bound to make some dangerous enemies. I've been attacked and shot at. I'd like to think that if someone tried to ambush me you'd be on the alert.''

Clint studied his old friend's handsome face. ''If anyone tries to kill you, they'll have to go through me first. Is that good enough for you?''

''Damn right it is!'' Rick said. ''That's all I wanted to know. So let's get out of here and go have some dinner! I got a place in mind that has French food that will drive you wild.''

''Sounds expensive.''

''I pay for everything, understand that?'' Rick said. ''You pay for nothing.''

Clint shook his head. ''I'll let you pay my dinner, but I won't be beholding to anyone for my meals and the board for my horse. I just don't feel right living off someone else.''

Rick was not pleased. ''All right,'' he growled. ''You always were too stiff backed and stubborn. But have it your own way. We got a lot to talk about and I think that what I have to say will prove to be very interesting to you, Clint. Very interesting indeed.''

''I'm all ears.''

''Honey,'' Rick said. ''It's gonna be time for you

to go back on stage again soon. Why don't you run along and let Clint and I talk business.''

''Aren't I invited to dinner?'' she pouted.

''Some other time,'' Rick said. ''Clint and I got man talk and a lot of catching up to do. Ain't that right, old buddy!''

''Sure do,'' Clint said, watching Miss Honey get up and leave without so much as a smile or a good-bye. ''Rick, I think you made her angry.''

''The hell with her,'' he replied. ''I'm her boss and she has to treat me right no matter if she's mad or not. Besides, I been seeing too much of her anyway. Miranda is getting angry.''

''Miranda?''

''Miss Miranda Hale,'' Rick said. ''My fiancée.''

''Oh,'' Clint said. ''I had no idea you were going to get married.''

''Well,'' Rick confessed. ''We haven't set a date and I'm in no hurry, but I guess I'm overdue for turning respectable. A businessman just can't be respectable with a woman like Miss Honey. No sir! Not even here on the Comstock.''

''Since when is being 'respectable' important to Rick Hadley?''

''I'd like to run for public office one of these days and then shoot for becoming a state senator. Maybe even the governor some day. There are plenty of folks who think I've got what it takes.''

''If what it takes is a good line of bullshit and a full set of white teeth,'' Clint said with a chuckle, ''then I guess you do have what it takes.''

Rick did not laugh but did manage a tight smile. ''What I always liked best about you was your honesty, Clint. Even as a boy, you always said exactly what was on your mind. A fella always knew where he stood with you, and I can see you haven't changed a bit in that respect."

"That's true," Clint said. "I remember when we played games for marbles or money that you would cheat, but then you'd always give the money back that you won. Do you still?"

"Still what?"

"Cheat and give the money back?"

Rick grinned wolfishly. "Let's go eat," he said. "We really have a lot of catching up to do."

Clint allowed himself to be led out a small door that took them through a narrow passageway and side door right near the main street. "I got a horse saddled at the hitching rail," he said.

"So do I," Rick said. "I always have a man keep a saddled horse ready and waiting."

Clint saw that Rick wasn't kidding. There actually was a horse saddled and waiting for him right close to Duke. And as they mounted and rode up the street heading for the French café, it gave Clint a lot of cause for worry. Why would a rich man like Rick always have a horse saddled and waiting?

The Gunsmith guessed that even though on the surface everything about Rick was as bright as gold, underneath the exterior Rick Hadley was a man with a lot of unpleasant things on his mind.

THREE

It was long after midnight when they left the French restaurant and rode their horses slowly over the divide and down into Gold Hill again.

"So you see," Rick said, "I got a little lucky by grubstaking a prospector and then buying out his claim cheap, and then turning it around and selling it for a hefty profit."

"Why didn't you work it yourself?" Clint asked. "You said it turned out to be worth hundreds of thousands of dollars."

"That's right, but in order to deep mine, you first have to have thousands of dollars to invest. I didn't have that much money. I can't tell you how often a man borrows and invests in hoisting equipment, mine cable, big steam engines and all the other stuff you need, then goes broke before he strikes the mother lode. It happens all the time. The only people who are getting rich on the Comstock are the ones that are already rich enough to invest whatever it takes to reach the ore way down under."

Clint said, "I had the feeling that you were getting pretty rich yourself."

Rick laughed. "Well, I am. At least rich by the average fella's standards. My brewery is profitable and so is my whorehouse."

"How many girls do you have working for you?" Clint asked.

"Five, if you count Miss Honey."

"She's a prostitute? I thought she was your big saloon draw."

"She's that too," Rick said. "But make no mistake about it, Miss Honey is as much a whore as any of the others on the Comstock, the only difference is, she's far more expensive. Charges about a hundred dollars a poke. Twenty times what the average whore charges. Needless to say, she doesn't lay down with any of the working men. Instead, she services the wealthy."

Clint had to hide a smile. "What the deuce can she do for a man that a five-dollar woman can't do?"

"You'll have to find out for yourself," Rick said. "She's pretty special."

"No woman's *that* special," Clint said. He took a deep breath. "But let's get back to you. I'm curious to know how you made your living before you had that stroke of good fortune."

"I was a gambler," Rick said. "I learned my profession on the Mississippi river boats. I killed a few men and that sort of ruined my reputation so I started west. Lived and gambled on San Francisco's Barbary Coast for several years. Those were wild times, my friend."

"Then the gold ran out?"

"That's right," Rick said. "By 1860 the California gold rush was history. Then, gold and silver were discovered here on the Comstock, and I joined the rush over the Sierras just like all the others without work in California. And like everyone else that I came with, I found out that all the good Comstock claims had already been taken. What was left wasn't worth the effort."

"But you grubstaked a prospector and bought his claim. How?"

Rick sighed. "His name was Waco Charlie Evans. He was old, wrinkled, and years of living alone and under the hot sun had made him crazy. But he could find gold. He made a strike down near Dayton. It was a good strike and since I had grubstaked him, I was entitled to half of the claim."

"Half?"

"Yeah," Rick said. "Only I wanted it all. I got Waco Charlie drunker than hell," Rick said. "Showed the dumb son of a bitch some assay reports that were really for another claim. He couldn't read and I told him that the reports said his claim was near to being worthless."

"So you cheated him out of a fortune," Clint said, his words sharp in their tone. "And then you sold the claim and invested it in a saloon and the rest is history."

"That's about the size of it. You see, I was burned out on gambling. You know as well as I do that if a fella doesn't quit the cards sooner or later his luck is going to run out. Most of the time he'll wind up getting shot to death by some drunken son of a bitch. There's no future in being a gambler. None at all."

"That's the same thing I decided about sheriffin'," Clint said. "I was—and I don't want to sound arrogant—but I was a first-rate lawman. Problem was I got this reputation as being the fastest gun on the frontier. That meant that I was the target of any young, would-be gunfighter. I killed more than a few before I realized that they'd just keep coming and coming. I'd had my fill of killing so I just gave up my badge and tried to put the past behind me."

"But you couldn't," Rick said.

"No," Clint admitted. "I took up the trade of gunsmithing but my reputation followed me wherever I went. I came to be known as the Gunsmith. Now, besides the gunsmithing, I play cards and pick up investigative work to keep myself solvent. That's what I was doing in Cheyenne when I got your letter. There were some cattle thieves and it took some time to gather the evidence. But I finally got it and made the arrest. A month ago, they were sentenced to twenty years in federal prison. It was a good job."

"I got a better job for you right here making more money than you ever dreamed possible," Rick said in a quiet voice. "I got a lot of enemies."

"Why?"

Rick craned his head back and stared up at the heavens. "You know, when a man starts to making real money, he always makes bad enemies. The way to the top is over your competitors. And then too, I'd be the first to admit that I'm pretty rough to work for. I don't tolerate slackness or petty thievery from my businesses. I deal with that sort of thing in the harshest way you could imagine. It discourages others from making the same kind of mistake."

"What exactly do you do?"

"I've cut off a man's fingers," Rick said without batting an eyelash. "Not all of them. Just their index fingers so they can't handle a gun very well."

Clint was amazed. "Pretty harsh treatment."

"How can you say that when you've killed what . . . a couple dozen men?"

"About that many," Clint admitted. "But they died in stand-up gunfights. I never had my men hold an enemy while I sliced off his fingers."

"Better a finger than his life," Rick argued. "Besides, what the hell difference does it make? What

I'm talking about is setting down rules for people to follow. When they break your rules, you got to discipline them or the rules aren't worth piss in a pond.''

Clint frowned. To him, it was one thing to kill in self-defense, quite another to cut off a man's fingers over the breaking of a rule or two.

''Look,'' Rick said. ''I've had some trouble lately with a couple of my competitors down in Gold Hill. There are two men in particular, Bill Meeker and Jim Banks who have sworn to have my hide tacked up on their saloon walls. I figure they aren't bluffing.''

''What would you have me do with them?''

''Kill them if they come near me,'' Rick said without hesitation. ''Both men are damned good with guns and both are plenty likely to hire professional help.''

''I see.''

Rick looked hard at him. ''Do you?''

''Yeah, and I'll help you through this.''

''Good! I knew I could count on you.''

''But,'' Clint added quickly. ''They'll have to make the first move. I won't just hunt them down and provoke a fight, if that's what you've got in mind.''

Rick frowned. ''Are you telling me that I'm going to have to wait until they make an attempt on my life before you'll do anything about Meeker and Banks?''

Clint expelled a deep breath. ''I'm afraid that's the way of it. Otherwise, I'm breaking the law. I could hang or go to prison for provoking a gunfight and killing those two. If you're really my friend, you'll understand that.''

Rick sighed. ''Sure, I understand. And you're absolutely right, of course. Besides, I'm pretty fair with a gun and I've got a few other good men on the payroll. It's not like I'm helpless or anything."

"Why don't you call a meeting and try and work out something?" Clint suggested. "Seems to me there's plenty of action for everyone up here. It's not like this town is in the grip of hard times. The money flows pretty good up here."

"It does for a fact," Rick said. "I'll tell you one thing, it's mighty good to have a friend that I can trust riding stirrup to stirrup with again. You got many friends?"

"I got a lot of acquaintances," Clint answered. "But not many good friends. I sometimes think that real friendships are formed early in a man's life at a time when he's less apt to be hiding behind some kind of image. At a time when life seems fun and everything is an adventure."

"I'd have to agree with that," Rick said. "After we grow up, men are so busy trying to outthink, outfight or outdo each other that there's no time or interest in real friendships. You're either looking up at someone that has more than yourself and wondering how to get to the next rung in the ladder, or looking down at those that have less and hoping they don't crawl over the top of you on their way up."

Clint clucked. "I don't quite see things like that," he said. "Most of my friends don't have much in the way of money. You're the wealthiest friend I have as a matter of fact. Money is important only when you don't have it. When you have it, it seems sorta trivial."

"Bullshit!" Rick said with a laugh. "I've got money and it don't seem a damn bit trivial."

"But it is," Clint argued, not expecting to change his old friend's mind but enjoying the intellectual banter. "I mean, if a man has a good horse, a good friend, enough jingle in his pockets for a meal and a drink, what else does he need?''

''Plenty. For instance, I can buy Miss Honey and you can't.''

''The hell with her,'' Clint snorted. ''I can find a woman who'll love me without reaching for a hundred dollar bill.''

''Sure you can, but she won't be as good,'' Rick said with a wink. ''And that is a fact.''

Clint smiled and rode on in silence. He decided that Rick was a man who had probably been corrupted by money, and it might take years before he sort of took a more balanced view on life. Maybe they never would see eye to eye when it came to money and what was important.

Hell, that was okay, too. A friend should never expect a friend to always share his point of view. In fact, a good strong difference of opinion often made friends closer if they didn't get too damn serious about things.

As they rode into the stable where Rick said they could keep their horses, the saloon owner said, ''Clint, I'm going to make you change your mind about money before you've been with me more than a week.''

''How do you propose to do that?'' Clint said with amusement.

''You wait and see. I got a plan in mind.''

Clint yawned. ''I've had a long day and covered a lot of miles. All that French wine and good food has sort of made me sleepy. I guess your instruction in the values of this world can wait awhile.''

But Rick winked. ''Don't bet on it.''

Clint discovered what his old buddy meant about two hours later when he was enjoying his sleep. One minute he was sawing logs and dreaming of casting a fishing line into the cold waters of nearby Lake Tahoe, and the next he was reaching for his gun as Miss Honey reached under the covers and began to massage his privates.

Clint's hand stilled on the butt of his six-gun and he blinked as if he was not sure he was awake or dreaming. But dreams didn't feel as real as Miss Honey did, and when she flipped the covers away from his body and took his manhood into her mouth, Clint was damn certain that he was awake.

"I haven't got close to a hundred dollars and even if I did, I sure wouldn't spend it all on one woman," he said, his voice still heavy with sleep.

Honey went, "Hmmmmm."

"What kind of an answer is that?"

She didn't reply but kept sucking and Clint leaned back and sighed. "Just as long as you're doing this for . . . hey, wait a minute! Rick is paying for you, isn't he!"

Honey lifted her head. The window was open and there was enough light from the street below to see that her lips were parted and glistening. She was wearing a silk wrapper which her breasts were pushing out of, and her face bore an almost feral expression that reminded Clint of a wild animal in heat.

"Yes," she whispered. "He is."

Clint lay back. "The man is trying to corrupt me with money," he decided out loud. "He's trying to prove his point and I don't like that."

Honey wasn't listening. Her lips and her tongue were doing wonderful things to Clint, and she was clearly enjoying her work. And despite his resolve to keep his mind off what she was up to, Clint felt himself stiffening.

"I liked your singing," he said. "But I didn't like

how when I gave you a compliment, you sort of took it for granted."

"Do you always let talk get in the way of pleasure?" she asked, raising her head.

Clint was flabbergasted but before he could reply, she was standing up and undressing; and when he saw how beautiful her body was, he got so distracted he even forgot her question. Then, she lifted her leg over his body and sat down on him slow and easy. Clint felt his wet tool slide easily into her, and it was wonderful when she sort of wiggled her bottom around and around.

"You're nice when you're quiet," she said. "You must be a very good friend of Rick's."

Clint swallowed and watched her as she began to bounce up and down a little so that her breasts waved, and he could hear little sucking sounds of their union. The sounds fired his passion, and he grabbed for her breasts, pulling her over him.

Honey laughed and let his tongue play with her nipples while her body kept bouncing up and down until they both began to lose all their good senses.

When Clint could stand what she was doing to him no longer, he grabbed and rolled her over onto her back and drove his manhood in and out of her with more energy than he thought he had left after such a long day and such little sleep.

"How long can you do this to me," she whispered raggedly. "You won't come too fast will you?"

"I'm going to screw you witless," he said with a smile. "I'm going to keep you under me until you beg for release."

"Hmmmm," she sighed. "If you can do that, I might just give Rick a refund and come back tomorrow night for more."

Clint growled like an animal as his hips worked at

her until she began to whimper like a puppy. He was enjoying himself more than he had with any woman for a long, long time.

Rick had been right about one thing—Honey was worth a whole lot more than the average whore. Maybe not twenty times, but enough so that a man would be willing to save his money for a shot at her once in a while.

"Oh, Clint!" she gasped, "I . . . I want to sing to you!"

The Gunsmith hesitated for a moment. "Sing?"

Without answer, Honey burst into a ribald and very popular frontier song called, "Honey, Let's Climb a Slippery Mountain and Slide on Down to Hell."

Clint reared up on his elbows and stared down at the woman who had him clamped rigidly between her lovely thighs. Her singing right into his face was distracting until her voice began to break apart and she started hitting all the high notes. But by then, Clint couldn't hear anything anyway.

FOUR

Clint slept until early afternoon, and when he awoke to a loud pounding at his door, Honey was gone. Clint reached for his gun and rubbed his eyes. "Who is it?"

"It's me, Rick! Open the damn door if you can still walk!"

Clint rolled out of bed and replaced his gun in his holster before he padded over to the door and unlocked it. When he opened the door, there Rick was, freshly shaven, dressed in an expensive black silk suit with a white shirt and black string tie. His boots were polished, and he looked scrubbed and ready to go out and hobnob with high society.

"Lordy, Lordy," Rick said, shaking his head at Clint who looked worn out and bedraggled. "I'd say from the looks of you that Honey really gave you a hundred dollars' worth of lovin' last night."

Rick's eyes were twinkling with mirth, and he looked to be enjoying Clint's discomfort and disreputable appearance so much that it was hard for him to keep from laughing out loud.

Clint scowled. "All right," he said. "You've had your show. Now why don't you go on down to the saloon and tend to your business while I pull myself together?"

Rick nodded. "I guess you probably don't want to

meet my fiancée, Miss Miranda Hale, today. If she saw your bloodshot eyes, she wouldn't form much of an opinion of your character.''

"Introductions can wait," Clint growled.

"Fair enough. I should tell you that she's the sheriff's daughter."

Clint was surprised. "I would have expected you to be fixin' to marry some high-society girl."

"Well, that was the original plan," Rick admitted. "Problem was, there are damn few of those around these parts, and not a one who would be seen with a man who owns a saloon and a whorehouse. As it is, Miranda doesn't know about the whorehouse or about Honey. And I'd expect that to remain a secret at least until after the wedding."

"I understand," Clint said, not really understanding how his friend could hide such a fact.

"And besides," Rick continued, "Miss Hale is prettier even than Honey and pure as the driven white snow."

Clint turned and shuffled back to collapse on the edge of his rumpled bed. He ran his fingers through his hair and yawned. "A woman like Honey would kill a man in a month if he had her every night. I thought she would never leave me to sleep. I lost count of the times we coupled. Even *I'm* sore!"

Rick burst out laughing. "That woman is a tigress and she'll screw your brains out. Did you get her to start singing?"

"Sure did," Clint said. "She sang every dirty song I ever heard, and a whole lot I never heard."

"You must have pleased her," Rick said. "Most fellas only get a couple of songs and that's about all they're up to anyway. But you just wait, old buddy. Right now you think maybe you're lucky to be alive and that you've had all of Honey that you want. But you're wrong. In a day, two at the most, she'll be on your mind constantly and you'll sell your soul for another night of her. I ought to know."

Clint took a deep breath and shook his groggy head. "I won't say you're wrong, but I'll have to wait and see about that. Right now, I feel like wadding fired out of a cannon."

"That'll pass with a couple of hours." Rick grinned knowingly. "I bet you're no longer trying to say that a whore is a whore."

"Honey isn't just a 'whore,' " Clint argued. "She's a screwing machine and a work of art. She's every man's fantasy only she's even more. Where on earth did you find her and why don't you make her an honest woman?"

Rick shrugged. "Because she's too much for any one man. It took me about three weeks of heaven and hell to figure that one out. During that time, I went through all the symptoms of a man that had been drugged and force-fed some kind of aphrodisiac. I lost thirty pounds and looked like an opium addict. I started to shaking and my muscles got weak and my rod got all red and swollen up the size of a big cucumber. I was a mess. We screwed so hard and often that all the hair around my cock got rubbed off, and that's when I knew that I had had enough."

"Whew!" Clint said. "I sure wouldn't want to go through all that."

"No man would, so don't feel ashamed of yourself." Rick hooked his thumbs into his gun belt. "But you know what?"

"What?"

"After I left her alone for about a week, I had to come back. Again and again and again. I still have to."

"What about Miss Miranda Hale? After you're

married, do you think that she's going to understand that?''

''Nope.''

''Well, then?''

Rick was a little annoyed. ''Well then, I guess I'll have to cheat on my wife in just the same way that I been cheating on her while she has been my fiancée. It's that simple.''

''It's never *that* simple,'' the Gunsmith argued, ''but it's your life and you have to decide.''

''Thanks,'' Rick said. ''For a minute there, I thought you were going to climb up on your pulpit and give me a sermon.''

Clint didn't even bother to reply to the sarcastic remark. Instead, he pulled on his pants and stood up. He stretched, burped up the taste of sour French wine and moved over to the window where he placed both hands on the frame and stared down into the street. ''If this is the good life,'' he drawled, ''I better go back to the simple life before I fall apart.''

Rick chuckled. ''I'll see you this evening over at the saloon. You'll want to hear Miss Honey sing, and you'll be back to your old self before you know it.''

Clint nodded, then listened to the door close. He walked over to the white porcelain wash basin and poured cold water into it from a chipped pitcher. He scrubbed his teeth with his forefinger until he smelled Miss Honey, and then he washed his mouth out with soap and splashed more water on his face and chest. With all that, it still took him several minutes to wake up, and then he unbuttoned the fly of his pants and studied his rod thoughtfully. It was a little red and definitely swollen. Well, it served him right. Miss Honey was an animal, and he'd have no more to do with her in order to preserve his own robust health.

"Who are you kidding?" he asked himself only a few minute later as he tied on his gun belt and looked into the mirror. "Rick has it right. That woman is worse than any narcotic. You'll want her again and again. She's a ball buster and a man killer. And she's worth every cent of her hundred bucks a night."

Clint left his hotel room and found his way to a hash house where he had a big steak and a bowl of chili, food that his stomach was more accustomed to digesting than the French cuisine that he had partaken the night before. Aware that he had only about forty dollars in this town where money flowed all too freely, Clint was dismayed to see the prices of food on the Comstock. He paid twice as much for his steak as he would have in Cheyenne, and, in truth, it was half the meat and tough as a cowhide.

"Three dollars for a steak like that is a little steep," he grumbled. "And the chili was greasy and mostly beans."

"Everything is greasy on the Comstock," the man who brought him the food said. "I don't like working here any better than you like eating here, so why don't we both agree not to see each other like this again?"

Clint was amused. "It's a deal. No tip, though."

"Fine," the waiter said. "If I were you, I wouldn't leave one either. That steak you ate was left over from some other fella's plate. At least you had good enough teeth to chew the damn thing."

The Gunsmith flushed with anger and dropped three dollars on the table. "That'll have to cover the chili and the beer as well."

"Fine with me," the waiter said, scooping up the

money, ripping off his apron and heading out the
door where he disappeared into the crowd.

"Damnedest place I ever had the misfortune to eat
at," Clint groused as he stepped outside, then headed
for Rick's saloon. "That fella probably just tied on
an apron a few minutes before I walked in and stole
my three dollars. I best find another eating place."

But as he marched along, he became aware that
there were very few eating places in Gold Hill. He
would have to ask Rick to give him some recom-
mendations or his stomach was going to rot.

Clint worked his tongue hard at a piece of meat
that had become lodged between his teeth. This
Comstock was rough on a man. Bad food and a
woman that would screw you into the grave. And
hell, he hadn't even met up with that surly freighter
who'd sworn to kill him after jumping off the man's
wagon as it barreled down the mountain. And there
was still the matter of Rick's enemies.

Clint patted the gun on his side. "If a bullet or
Honey ain't the death of me, bad food or whiskey
will be."

As Clint marched along, slowly weaving his way
through the crowds that always seemed to congest
the boardwalks, he decided that he had better tread
lightly until he got the lay of things on the Comstock
Lode. He was not wet behind the ears when it came
to hard towns and fast women, but mostly, he'd
been accustomed to cow towns instead of mining
towns. And there was a big difference.

A mining town was sort of crazy. It was built in a
frenzy with the full knowledge that every strike ran
out and that a man had to take what he could get as
fast as he could get it. To Clint's way of thinking,
miners were a queer lot anyway. A lot of them were
foreigners. The Welsh were everywhere here on the

Comstock because they were the world's best and most experienced deep miners. They were joined by a lot of other nationalities, Irish, English, and Scots, being the most prevalent, but there was also a healthy number of Mexicans, French and Basque. On the whole, they were hard drinking and hard fighting sons of bitches who seemed to transfer their frustrations directly from the mines to the saloons.

The Gunsmith didn't really understand miners, and he was leery of them. But cowboys, now they were a different breed altogether. They fought, sure. But they were a fraternity. They understood each other's lingo, and they spoke the same words and saw things pretty much in the same light. You could reason with a cowboy, and during his years as a lawman, Clint had reasoned with many of them. And if you wanted to strike up a conversation with a cowboy, that was the easiest thing in the world. All you had to do was ask him about his horse or his outfit or what he thought about cattle, the damned barbed wire slowly beginning to creep south from Iowa, or about the new English breeds of cattle like the Hereford. Why, there was not a cowboy in the West who would not be able to talk for hours without interruption on his beloved longhorn cattle or his favorite types of saddle, riata or breed of stock.

But miners, hell, you never knew what they wanted to talk about or even if they spoke your language. The only safe talk was about women and whiskey, but those topics got sort of limiting after awhile. Miners were often men who had left their homelands to come to America to strike it rich and then return wealthy. Only, Clint had never met one that seemed to be advancing that original plan.

Miners were always looking forward to tomorrow

when they'd strike it rich. Cowboys were much more content with living today.

"Hey you!"

Clint turned on his heel as he felt himself being spun around, and be damned if he wasn't staring right in the face of that red-bearded freighter that he had sort of been on the watch for. Only now, it was a little too late to take evasive measures, and before Clint's hand could reach his gun, the freighter's huge fist was smashing into his jaw and sending him backpeddling off the sidewalk. He hit on his ass and slid three more feet until he came to rest against a water trough.

"I'm gonna tear your goddamn head off!" the freighter roared, jumping off the boardwalk with blood in his eyes.

Clint rolled sideways and the freighter's momentum carried him headlong into the trough. A crowd of bored miners perked right up, and when the red-bearded giant tried to straighten, Clint booted him in the butt and sent him toppling back into the trough.

"Tell him I'll be around," the Gunsmith said as he dodged into the nearest saloon, moved through the crowd and then found the back door to the alley. It wasn't that he was afraid of the freighter because he could always shoot the overgrown bastard, it was just that he was still feeling a little punky from last night's debauchery; and he needed time to recover. Besides, he sure didn't want to trade punches with the man, and if he put a bullet through him he might have to go to jail and plead self-defense. That would mean that his name would probably be picked up by the local newspaper, and then any element of surprise he might have had to use against Rick's enemies would be lost.

Much better, Clint reasoned as he hurried up the

alley, took a side street and worked his way to Rick's saloon to sort of put the matter of that red-bearded giant aside for now and get his bearings. Besides, Clint thought as he rubbed the numb side of his face, the man had gotten in one hell of a punch and that just might satisfy him enough to drop the matter entirely.

It might, but Clint very much doubted it.

FIVE

Rick was not in the saloon when Clint arrived, but Honey was resting back in that little alcove behind the bouncers and the red felt rope. Clint was working his jaw, trying to keep it from locking up on him when he spotted her and she called his name.

Clint was too much a gentleman not to respond. It would have been cruel to spurn Honey in front of her adoring fans, and it might even have been a little dangerous. With a deep sigh, he forced a lopsided grin and moved over to the felt rope.

"Hi there," he said between the bouncers who scowled at him.

"Hi, Clint!" In sharp contrast to himself, Honey looked as fresh as the morning dew. It depressed Clint to see how rested she appeared and the depression momentarily robbed him of his famed wit so that he could think of nothing to say in greeting.

Finally, Honey said, "Why don't you come on in here and join me? We can have a drink or two."

Clint shrugged. He looked up into the face of the bouncer whose balls he had flattened with his knee less than twenty-four hours earlier and said, "Do I have to give you the password again, or will you let me through this time?"

"I'm gonna break your fuckin' neck before this is over," the man snarled under his breath.

Clint refrained from slamming his heel down on the man's foot and then making an all-out attempt to plaster his nose across his meaty face. "You keep saying that to me and I keep ignoring you. One of these days, I'm going to have to take you seriously."

The bouncer flushed and his hands formed into knots but Honey said, "Frankie, don't you dare hit him or I'll have Rick fire you!"

Frankie shuddered uncontrollably, but he allowed Clint to pass into Rick's private little alcove.

As soon as Clint eased into the booth next to Honey, she noticed his bruised and rapidly swelling face and said, "Oh, my! That didn't happen last night, did it!"

"No," he groused. "I'm swollen up below the belt from last night, but this is from a man's fist."

She linked her arm through his and ordered them each double whiskies. "Rick told me you were always a man of action. After last night, I am inclined to agree with him."

Clint had to laugh out loud, but the laugh sounded hollow, even to himself. "Well, I'm about actioned out for now. Tell me, are you human?"

Honey giggled. "Why, you ought to know the answer to that one! Of course I am."

"You must come from Viking stock," he said.

"Are you complaining, or what?"

It was obvious that he had injured her feelings and, since that was not his intention, Clint relaxed and said, "I didn't mean anything unkind, Honey. I just never met anyone quite as . . . well, physical as you are in bed."

She shrugged. "Did you like the way I sang to you in the dark?"

"I sure did," he lied. "I can still remember the words to some of those new songs. They were the raunchiest lines I ever did hear."

"Men like to hear them when we screw. It seems to make them even more passionate."

"I see."

The whiskies came and Clint drank his down neat, then ordered another for each of them. The drinks were a dollar each, but Rick served better than average liquor and Clint wasn't complaining. The double had eased the throbbing he felt on one side of his face and in his sore rod.

He watched Honey sip her drink and said, "Tell me you don't do that every night."

"Naw," she said. "Only once or twice a week. Mostly, I'm Rick's woman and he knows how to slow things down a little so they're nice and easy. I guess he's trying to calm himself down for when he marries that Hale girl."

The way she said "Hale girl" left little doubt in Clint's mind that Honey was not one bit pleased with Rick's engagement. "I take it you don't like her."

"You've got that right," Honey snapped. "She's just a little lily-white faker. Rick thinks she's a virgin, but I've heard enough to know she's slept with a few men. He thinks she's something special, but he's going to be in for a real surprise when he climbs between her legs."

Clint did not want to hear anymore slander. "Tell me what you know about Rick's enemies. He said something about a couple of men named Bill Meeker and Jim Banks that own a saloon in competition with this one. Are they the kind who would kill Rick or hire someone else to kill him?"

"I don't know," Honey said. "They might think that Rick intends to see them dead so they'd want to kill him first."

Clint frowned. "Would Rick really have them killed first?"

"Well of course he would! How do you think he got rid of Dave Fartley?"

"Who was Dave Fartley?"

"His partner, of course. Dave was the one that originally owned this saloon. He got into some money trouble and Rick made him a loan for half interest in this place. About six months later, no Dave Fartley."

"What do you mean?"

"I mean," Honey said, leaning close so that they could not possibly be overheard, "that the man just disappeared."

"Sometimes that happens," Clint said.

"Well not to a man like Fartley. He lived and breathed this saloon. He slept here, ate here, did it all here. He'd never have just walked away. He was murdered."

"Rick wouldn't do that!"

"I didn't say it was Rick!" she exclaimed, her face reflecting shock. "Oh no I didn't!"

"Calm down," Clint said. "All right, if it wasn't Rick, who was it?"

"One of those big bastards standing there," Honey said. "They work for Rick. I bet they thought that killing Fartley was what was expected of them. Anyway," she added, sipping her drink, "that's my theory."

Clint shook his head. "If I were you, I'd keep my theory all to myself. That kind of talk can be fatal."

"Hell, I know that! It could also get a girl married."

Now Clint understood what Honey was driving at. "You're playing a reckless and stupid game if that's what you have in mind," he warned. "I think you'd be better off to forget the whole thing and just walk away from it."

"Not me," she said. "I been giving it to Rick free for almost a year now while he drools and moons over that Hale girl. I have an investment in Rick.''

His face lit up. ''Yeah, that's a good way to put it. An investment.''

Clint drank his second whiskey. ''Tell me about Rick's other enemies. I need to know what I'm getting myself into before I go any farther with this. And the better I can protect him, the more chance you might have of cashing in on your 'investment.' Understand what I'm saying?''

''Sure I do. But you're not going to like what I tell you.''

''Why?''

''Because Rick has more enemies than I could name. He's climbed over dozens of men to get to where he is right now. There are plenty of people that would like to see him dead.''

''You almost sound like you're one of them,'' Clint blurted.

''I am not!'' Honey studied her hands and then she reached under the table and rubbed Clint's thigh and then his crotch until he felt himself stir painfully.

''Cut it out,'' he said roughly. ''We're talking about something damned important here.''

She pulled her hand away quickly. ''Rick is a hard man,'' she said. ''And all right, there are times when I wish he was dead. He's beat the hell outa me before and he will again. Beat me so bad I couldn't get up on his damned stage and sing for a week.''

Clint rocked back on his seat. ''I find that hard to believe.''

''Believe whatever you want to, Clint. But it's the truth.''

The news depressed Clint and he said with a shake of his head, ''When I knew Rick, he wasn't mean at all. He was kind to women and sympathetic to most everyone that was down and out.''

"Well, whoopee for him as a boy!" Honey said. "But he grew up entirely different. I know him better than anyone, and he has a mean streak a foot wide going up and down his backbone. But he's also got a good streak. He can be a son of a bitch one minute and the nicest guy you'd ever want to meet the very next. Rick gives a pretty fair amount of money to charity. If there's a mine cave-in, he's right there with a pick and a shovel and a bag of money for the widows and their children."

"I was wondering when you were going to tell me what you like enough about him to want to get married."

"Well, you just heard it," Honey said. "I think I can handle Rick if he don't get himself killed or hung. He wants to build another saloon and then I think he'll stop driving himself so hard. But that Hale girl will be his ruin."

"Why?"

"Because," Honey said, getting up to sing, "she expects an honest man, though she has no reason to because her father is as crooked as a dog's hind leg. Rick will never be entirely honest. And someday, he'll lose his famous temper and beat the hell out of her too."

Clint looked down at his drink and then finished it. When he looked back up again, Honey was being escorted through the crowd, and the miners were stomping and yelling with anticipation.

Clint left the booth and shouldered his way to the bar where he ordered beer. He tossed it down and ordered another. He was feeling sort of low and knew he could drink all night, but the beer would not wash away the bad taste in his mouth.

SIX

It wasn't until three days later that Clint was finally allowed to meet Miss Miranda Hale, and if it had not been for accidentally bumping into her as she exited the sheriff's office, the meeting might not have taken place for no telling how long.

"Excuse me!" Clint said, tipping his hat and bowing just a little the way his mother had once taught him to do out of politeness. "You're so pretty, you'd have to be Miss Miranda Hale."

The woman was about twenty, with long auburn hair and a complexion that was like peaches and cream. "I don't believe we have been introduced," she said, starting to move around him.

"No we haven't," Clint said. "And one look at you tells me why. My best friend Rick must be a little bit jealous, or he'd have introduced us days ago."

She stopped, then turned, "You are Clint Adams, the famous Gunsmith!"

He removed his black Stetson hat and tried to look his most harmless. "I am honored to finally make your acquaintance."

She had freckles on her cheeks and teeth as perfect as Rick's. She was slender enough that she gave the impression of being willowy and fragile, though Clint was sure she was not. A fragile, retiring girl would not have been able to attract Rick.

"My, my," she said. "Rick has told me so much about you and he when you were boys. And then when he said you had come to visit, I wondered when we would meet."

Clint grinned. "Oh, sooner or later he'd have gotten around to introducing us even if I had to twist his arm up behind his back. But I'm glad that it happened now."

Clint looked at the packages she was holding. "Here," he said, "let me help you carry them."

"But they're really not very . . ."

Clint took the packages. "I guess you were probably just stopping by to say hello to your father."

"Yes," she said, looking a little surprised by his politeness. "I should like to introduce you to him. You're one of his heroes."

Clint would just as soon meet the sheriff some other time but Miranda was already pushing the door open and stepping into the sheriff's office. The place was clean but disorderly. Clint, having been a lawman many years, figured he could size up a lawman pretty well with one glance around his office. What he saw in Gold Hill added up to a sheriff who had more interest in reading dime novels and newspapers than he did in policing his town. The rifle rack was almost empty, and the weapons leaning in it were outmoded old single shots. The Wanted Posters were yellowing and obviously out of date, and the jail had a stack of boxes packed with worn dime novels. The cell gave Clint the impression it was rarely occupied.

"Father, this is the Gunsmith."

Clint turned to regard a fiftyish, jowly man in a red flannel shirt and baggy brown pants, who hadn't bothered to pin on his badge and wasn't even wearing a side arm. Sheriff Hale looked more like a retired grocer than an active lawman. He was reading a dime novel, but when Clint's nickname was given, he dropped the novel and stood up fast.

"I heard you were in Gold Hill," he said, his face breaking into a wide grin. "I sure was planning to look you up soon and maybe swap some lawman's stories with you."

Hale glanced at his daughter and puffed himself up a little with self-importance. "Us lawmen got a lot in common."

I doubt it, Clint thought as he reached down and picked up the dime novel whose title was, *Lawman of the Wild, Wild Plains.*

Sheriff Hale flushed a little with embarrassment. "It's amazing how much nonsense them books have in 'em. Why, if Wild Bill Hickok and Buffalo Bill and fellas like you and Kit Carson did all that those dime novel writers said that you did, why, you'd have to have more than the nine lives of a cat!"

The sheriff laughed at his own exaggeration and Clint managed to dredge up a self-depreciating chuckle.

The sheriff hurried into his cell and began opening boxes and grabbing books. "I got at least a half dozen of 'em that are based on what you did in Texas, Colorado, Arizona and New Mexico. They say you are faster with a gun than John Wesley Hardin ever was."

Clint looked around feeling suddenly very uncomfortable in this place. He did not want to see a bunch of dime novels glorifying himself or any other lawman. To him, wearing a badge had always been a tough but sacred business. You never shot a man except when you had to, and then you did it to kill. You didn't wear two guns, and you didn't fan your hammer or do any of the other silly things that people believed after reading dime novels.

"There's no glory in being a lawman," Clint said. "I'd just as soon not see any of those books if it's all the same to you, Sheriff."

Hale stood up quick and the books tumbled out of his hands to fall on the jail floor. For a moment, he looked stunned. "But . . . but these I grabbed are all about you, Mr. Adams!"

Clint had no wish to embarrass anyone further so he decided it was time to leave. "I better scoot along," he said lamely, pushing the packages back into Miranda Hale's arms. "I'm sorry."

He was out the door and starting down the boardwalk when she caught up with him and said, "You were pretty rude to my father!"

Clint slowed his pace. "I didn't mean to be," he said in a terse voice. "In fact, given what I saw in there, I thought I was as charitable as a man could expect."

"What's that supposed to mean?" Miranda demanded.

Clint stopped, then pulled the young woman out of the path of the crowd and shoved his hands deep into his pockets. "What the hell is a man like that doing in a sheriff's office?"

"Why . . . why my father was elected sheriff by a landslide during the last election!"

"Figures," Clint drawled. "Bet that's because he never does anything and, therefore, he never makes any enemies."

Her jaw dropped and her blue eyes flashed. "Why . . . why you're just awful, aren't you! Are you mad because of the fact that my father has managed to uphold the law without killing one single human being! Is that what has you so upset when you compare it to your own bloody past?"

Clint's own anger melted under her stare. "I'm

sorry," he said wearily. "What I saw and what I think your father is or isn't has no importance at all. The only thing that matters is that you are my best friend's bethrothed and I've insulted you, though that was surely not my intention. Will you forgive me?"

She was pretty when angry and even prettier when she offered him a forgiving smile. "Here," she said, pushing the packages at Clint. "You offered to help me carry them home, so I accept your offer—and your apology."

"I should have looked at those dime novels he was so proud of," Clint said. "I guess I really did hurt his feelings."

"Yes, you did. But I don't understand why."

"It's just that any man who is sheriff of a town as wild as this has no business reading such nonsense and believing all the silly, ridiculous things in those books. It could be dangerous for him, and for others. He's old enough to know that those books are a waste of time. They're written for easterners. People who want to think that the West is wild and romantic and filled with all sorts of crazy bad men and outlaws and heathen Indians just waiting for the guy in the white hat to shoot them dead."

Miranda studied him closely. "You're not wearing a white hat, Mr. Adams. And you're not one bit what I thought you'd be."

"I might as well take that as a compliment instead of an insult," Clint said philosophically.

"Yes, why don't you," she told him as she linked her arm through his and led him down the boardwalk. "We go left here on Raymond Street. Father and I live just a half block up this hillside. See that white house with the white picket fence?"

"Who could miss it with all those roses planted

along the front?'' Clint asked. ''You can sure tell wherever a woman lives.''

What Clint meant was that there were thousands of tents and old shacks dotting the slopes, but wherever a woman lived, you could see a touch of love, of beauty. There'd be a few flowers, maybe a painted fence or some other little sign of gentleness that was entirely lacking among the bachelor tents and shacks.

When they reached the picket fence gate, Miranda opened it and walked up to a small front porch where she asked Clint to put the packages down. ''You just sit in one of those rocking chairs while I go inside and bring us out something cool to drink.''

''I should probably be running along,'' he said.

''Can't you stay just a few minutes and talk?''

She really seemed to want him to stay, so Clint nodded. Ten minutes later, they were both sipping tea and rocking back and forth. The day was warm but there was a breeze that cooled the air, and they had a fine view of the Comstock. Behind them stood mighty Sun Mountain where the main body of ore seemed to originate and on whose slopes rested the queen of the Comstock, Virginia City. Clint could also see a graveyard with its silent sentinels of stone which were a mute testimony to the hardships that men endured to find gold and silver. And all around them were mining claims marked by piles of tailings that grew each day and measured a man's progress into the barren hillsides.

''I never tire of looking out at these mountains and watching the men work. I watch them winter, spring, summer and fall. They are tireless and never seem to lose hope, but so few ever strike any paying ore.''

''One thing I would not become is a miner,'' Clint said. ''I never got bit by the gold bug, and I don't like the feel that the underground gives a person. It's the hardest life I've ever seen.''

''I feel the same way,'' Miranda said, her eyes distant. ''I guess that's one of the things I like most about Rick. He doesn't have any intention of ever owning a mine.''

''Rick is too smart for that. He mines the pockets of the miners.''

Miranda looked sharply at him. ''That is not a very complimentary way of putting it,'' she said. ''I like to think that Rick is simply providing a form of recreation for those hard working men. God knows they have so little joy in their existence. I think Rick is doing a kindness to provide some entertainment and relaxation.''

Clint nodded. ''That's a nice way to look at it, Miss Hale. And I'm sure that you are correct.''

''Your words say one thing, your voice says another. What's wrong?''

''Nothing.'' Clint figured it was about time to leave. For some reason, he was bound and determined to dig himself into a heap of trouble with this girl who seemed to be able to read his troubled heart and mind. He just could not get past the fact that this girl was so naive about the man she was to marry. Why didn't her own father at least tell her that Rick owned a whorehouse and slept almost every day with Miss Honey? Didn't Sheriff Hale even give a damn about the fact that his daughter's heart would be broken when she eventually learned of these things? What kind of a father was he!

These and other similar questions disturbed the Gunsmith so much that he had to get up and leave. He placed his cup and saucer of tea down beside his rocking chair and pushed himself to his feet. ''I

better be going, Miss Hale. I do have some things
that need attending to."

She stood up, surprised and obviously disappointed,
but determined to smile. "I had hoped that we would
have a little more time to visit. I think it's important
that a man's best friend and his wife-to-be get better
acquainted. After Rick and I are married, I would
think that you would come often to our home for
supper and socializing."

"I might not stay on the Comstock too long," he
said, making the decision out loud. "I just might
ride on in a week or two. You see, I'm sort of
rootless. A drifter."

"Oh. Well," she said, "I'm sorry to hear that. I
had the impression from Rick that you and he might
even become partners in the new saloon that he is
getting ready to start up in Virginia City. I know he
was counting on your help."

"Did he tell you what kind of help I am supposed
to provide?"

Miranda looked puzzled. "No. I just assumed that
you would have some role in policing the tables and
the games to keep them honest. Also, with your
reputation, I'm sure there would be much less likeli-
hood of ruffians causing trouble."

She frowned. "Am I correct? Is that the sort of
thing that Rick had in mind for you?"

Clint did not want to tell her that he was needed as
Rick's personal gunfighter and protector. That Rick
was afraid for his own life and had more enemies
than friends, and that he lived with an element of
fear.

"Yeah," the Gunsmith said. "Something like that,
I guess. I'll see you around, Miss Hale. Thanks for
the tea and your company."

When he reached the gate, she called, "Can you

and Rick come here for dinner tomorrow evening? I'll fix you something special, and maybe we can get off to a better start."

Clint paused, then turned and said, "I'd like that, Miss Hale. But I had better let the invitation ride until some later date. I'm pretty busy these days and I hope you understand."

Her shoulders dipped with frustration. "But I don't understand at all!" she cried. "What is wrong with me!"

"Not a damn thing," he said quietly, "and I guess that's the entire problem in a nutshell."

SEVEN

When Clint returned to Rick's Saloon, a troubled storm was brewing deep inside him and his mood was in sharp contrast to the laughter and riotous drinking that surrounded him.

He pushed a little too roughly through the boisterous crowd of miners and angled toward the bar, ignoring the private alcove where Rick might be waiting. "A whiskey," he shouted.

Heads turned and miners glared because, up on the stage, Miss Honey was singing and dancing and the miners felt that any conversation above a whisper was disrespectful. Clint got his whiskey and tossed it down, and then he banged his glass hard on the bar for another.

Miss Honey looked over the sea of faces and their eyes locked. The miners assumed she was annoyed, but she wasn't. She could tell at a glance that the Gunsmith was upset and that bothered her, made her forget her lines and loose her place in the song.

Her momentary confusion was well noted by the audience who supposed that Clint was entirely to blame. "Mister, you damn sure better not make any more noise while that angel is singing for us," a bull-shouldered miner said in a heavy German accent.

The bartender said, "If you're smart, you'll take your foul mood somewhere else before it gets you in a bunch of trouble."

"And if you're smart," Clint said evenly, "you'll just pour my drink and keep your advice to yourself."

The bartender didn't appreciate being talked to that way, but he poured before he moved on down the bar and whispered something derogatory about Clint to several of his regular customers who glared at the Gunsmith with unconcealed challenge in their eyes. Most of them were dirty, powerful men whose muscles were as hard as wood from swinging a pick or shovel ten hours a day. Men who worked down under the Comstock were tough and they were brave. Picking a fight was not a thing they shied away from.

Clint wasn't aware of anyone. He didn't hear Miss Honey's voice, and he didn't notice the hard looks he was getting from everyone surrounding him. His dark thoughts being torn apart as he considered what was to him a major moral dilemma. He was being ripped between a sense of loyalty for his blood brother and also a sense of honor and duty to inform Miss Hale that she was being set up for a husband who would break her pure and trusting heart.

Hell, maybe it was all none of his business, but he wasn't the kind of man who could just stand aside and watch someone like Miranda be destroyed. If she had been told the truth, and then, like Honey, had decided Rick was still worth the game, that was fine. But Miranda, for some reason, hadn't a clue about the true nature of the man she was going to marry. Hadn't the least idea that he was a cheat, that he might have murdered his ex-partner, that people said he ran crooked card games and that he had wanted Clint to kill his enemies on sight.

And yet, Rick was his blood brother. His childhood best friend.

"Son of a bitch!" Clint muttered. "I gotta get off the Comstock before . . ."

"Hey!" the German miner growled, grabbing the front of Clint's shirt. "I told you to keep quiet."

Clint exploded with all the pent up fury and confusion that had been building inside him since he'd left Miranda. Without an instant's hesitation, he drove the sole of his boot down the miner's shinbone, peeling away flesh and hair. It was an old trick and one that was almost as painful as a knee administered to the crotch.

The German's round face contorted in pain. His mouth formed an "O" and he sucked in a deep breath. Clint stepped back and filled the "O" with his knuckles. He put everything he had into the punch, knowing that he had better get his best lick into the fight early because the German was bigger and stronger than he was.

The miner's front teeth were knocked loose and he was hurled backward and half way up the bar. Dazed, lips and teeth broken, he shook his head, and then he roared with a mixture of pain and anger.

A good fight was the only thing that was better than watching Miss Honey. Miners pushed back until a circle was formed. The German eased off the rim of the bar. His round-toed work boots thumped on the floor boards. "I'm gonna break your back," he growled.

"At least you got a fresh line," Clint said, backing up slightly and setting himself for the charge that he knew was coming. The German was going to try to snap Clint's spine. Looking at the man's bloodied face, Clint was sure that he could succeed if given the chance.

The miner charged. Clint ducked under his outstretched arms and drove a wicked uppercut to his kidney as he passed. Everyone in the saloon heard the man's sharp intake of breath and noted it was followed by an involuntary groan of pain.

The miner was caught by his friends. They glared at Clint, for he was a stranger. "Get him Jon! Kill him!"

Jon shook off the pain like a terrier shaking off water. He growled and charged again, only this time he bent low and came in hard and fast. There was no chance to duck, and so Clint planted his feet and bashed him in the nose. But Jon's nose had been broken many times and it did not even slow him down when Clint's fist broke it again. He simply came on and when his arms wrapped around the Gunsmith, he bellowed in triumph. He locked his hand around his wrist and heaved Clint off his feet.

It was like being cut in half with a piece of barbed wire. Clint grabbed a fistful of hair and bent back the German's head and hammered it bloody, but the back-breaking grip just kept tightening until the Gunsmith could not breathe. Could not even think for the pain.

Dimly, he could hear shouts and knew that the spectators were all against him and that either his rib cage or his spine was going to snap and it was only a matter of which one went first.

With his brain on fire, Clint tried to hook his thumbs into Jon's eyes, but the German was too experienced for that and buried his forehead against Clint's chest and his bull neck was much too strong to bend back.

Clint grabbed the man's ears, and with his mind starting to lose contact with reality, he did the only thing that he figured would save his life—he bit the German's ear off and spit it out at the crowd with the full intention of biting the other ear off if he lived long enough.

The reaction was instant and more than he could have ever hoped for. One minute he was dying, the very next the powerful miner was throwing him aside and lunging for his missing ear. Clint sagged to the floor, and even the hardened miners were so shocked that they did not react for a full three seconds. Then, they piled on the Gunsmith, smashing him with fists and feet.

With his mind swamped with pain, Clint barely heard Honey's voice as she cried out and threw herself from the stage to grab a man's gun and start filling the saloon's ceiling with bullet holes.

"Get off of him!" she screamed as she kept pulling the trigger. "Let him alone!"

No one except the revered Honey, not even Rick himself, could have stopped the miners from beating Clint to death. Sullen and cursing, the miners pulled back from the battered gunfighter as Honey knelt at his side, the smoking six-gun still in her fist.

"Get a doctor!" she yelled.

No one moved.

"I said get a doctor!"

The miners stood resolute. "He bit off Jon's ear. We should have killed him. What are you doing this for? He was making noise while you sang!"

"I didn't mind!"

Another big German stepped out from the circle of angry miners. "So you chose him over one of us?"

"Yes!"

"Then you take him and you never come back here in this place to sing!"

Heads bobbed up and down in disagreement. Honey looked at the men, and then she helped Clint to his feet. He was still conscious, still aware of what was going on. "Why didn't you use your gun?" she asked.

" 'Cause," he mumbled. "Wouldn't have been a fair fight."

Honey looped one of Clint's arms over her shoulder.

"Get out of here!" the miners shouted in unison. "Get out of here!"

Honey half carried, half dragged Clint out of the saloon, and when they reached the nearest horse trough, she eased his bloodied face into the water until it was completely submerged. He came up slowly, but at least his head was cleared and the fresh night air roused him back to the present.

"Why," he asked in a thick voice, "did you save my life and ruin your own livelihood?"

Honey sat down on the edge of the trough. "I don't know," she said, not quite in belief that she had acted the way she had. "I just didn't want to see a man that I'd had such a good night with beaten to death by a drunken bunch of miners. I guess I like you, Clint. That's just as plain, simple and dumb a reason as I can give."

He hauled himself out of the trough. "My face feels like it's been run over by an ore wagon. I've never been punched so many times in my life."

She supported him. "We better get you to your room."

Clint nodded. He knew he was a mess. His shirt was torn half off, and what was still hanging to him in rags was bloodied. "I'm not going to be able to hurry," he said, breathing in short bursts through a nose that felt broken or at least packed with blood.

"I'm in no hurry," Honey said. "I've got nothing more to do tonight but help you."

Bent over with pain and moving with great difficulty, Clint managed to get back up on the boardwalk. With Honey under his arm, he guessed he could make it to his hotel even though every step was a torment.

Suddenly, Rick and Miranda Hale came into view.

They were just strolling along together as if they were in Boston or someplace refined where people did that sort of thing. The moment she saw them, Honey froze with indecision. She wanted to run but knew that she could not leave Clint to himself.

"I'm sorry," Clint whispered, reaching out to grab a porch post and trying to straighten himself up. "Go ahead and get out of here."

"No," Honey said.

"My God!" Rick called, finally noticing them and rushing forward. "What in the hell happened to you! Who did this!"

Honey swallowed. She looked at Miranda and then down at her feet. "There was a bad fight in your saloon, Mr. Hadley."

"In my saloon? Clint, what's she talking about!"

"I took on a miner and bit his ear off before he broke my back," Clint gasped. "His friends took that rather unkindly and decided to stomp my brains out on your floor. Honey saved my life when she grabbed a gun and opened fire. That's about the size of it."

"You shot up my saloon!"

"Only the ceiling," Honey said, her voice pleading for understanding. "I didn't hit any of the chandeliers or anything."

"Son of a bitch!" Rich swore with exasperation. "You're supposed to work for me, not against me! Those miners are my bread and butter."

Clint ground his teeth as a spark of fury kindled and flared. "It was a fair fight, Rick! When the German came at me, I was fighting for my life. Hurting your business was not the main thing on my mind."

"Well you had no damned right to cause trouble in there. And you," Rick said, swinging around and slapping Honey across the face so hard that she staggered. "Not only will I have to pay someone to fix the ceiling and the roof, but now you're probably all washed up in my club. What am I supposed to do about that!"

Miranda's hand flew to her mouth. "Rick! Get ahold of yourself!"

"Shut up!"

Clint pulled himself up to his full height. Every breath was a struggle, but he felt more anger than pain when he saw the trickle of blood leaking out of the corner of Honey's mouth. "You ever strike her again," he rasped, "and blood brother or not, I'll see you buried."

The threat was spoken quietly, yet that made it seem all the more deadly. Rick was brought up short. He looked at Miranda, then at Honey and finally at Clint. "Clint, you and I are going to have to reach a better understanding tomorrow," he said in a trembling voice. "I've got enough trouble from my enemies without having to worry about what kind of shit my friends are throwing at me. We're going to have a talk first thing in the morning."

"Yeah," Clint gritted. "I think that's one hell of a fine idea. Honey, let's go."

She helped him walk away from Rick and Miranda, whose face was numb with shock, and who was now staring at her fiancé with an incredulous expression touched with loathing.

Clint didn't give a damn. He had seen the real man his blood brother had become. And what he saw he did not like one damn bit.

EIGHT

Rick was in a depressed but confident mood the following morning when he tapped on Clint's door. His depression deepened, however, when Honey opened the door and let him inside. Her lip was swollen up, and Rick was reminded that he had slapped her very hard last night. Even worse, he'd slapped her in front of Clint and Miranda. That had been an unforgivable indiscretion and one that would cost him dearly in Clint's and Miranda's eyes.

The room was dim, but Rick could still see the battered face of the Gunsmith. He should have been more sympathetic last night. From what his bartender and other employees had related of the fight, Clint had uncharacteristically been asking for trouble, but still Rick should have been more sympathetic. Something had set him off and Rick guessed that maybe Clint had had an argument with Honey or someone and had taken his anger into the saloon.

On the other hand, Honey had spoken the truth. Her bullet holes had not even gone through his ceiling. They'd be easy to patch, and the roof wasn't in danger of leaking in the winter. The real damage had been that Honey was now viewed by the miners as a betrayer, and that attitude was going to be tough to handle, if it could be handled at all. Those kind of men did not forget disloyalties and they were not forgiving people. The hell with it! He was going to take her and his business up and over the divide into Virginia City. He was going big time at last.

"Morning," he said, pulling up a chair beside Clint's bed. "I guess I sure do owe you and Honey an apology."

When Clint just stared at him, Rick shook his head with dismay. "Listen, I just lost my head last night. I have an awful temper. You remember I had it even when we were kids. I never quite learned how to handle it. When I get mad, I lose my head sometimes and say things . . . do things that I regret. I'm sorry."

Clint pushed himself up on his pillow. He wasn't sure what to do. His body ached all over, but a careful examination by the doctor that Honey had brought in last night had assured him that he had no broken bones. Just a bunch of bruises and knots on his head and his body. It had been a long, long time since Clint had been knocked to the floor and had a mob work him over like that. Clint vowed that it would never happen again. One well-placed boot in the head and a man might either die, or be brain damaged for life.

"Clint," Rick pleaded. "I said I was sorry. I *mean* it. I'll do anything to make up for the way I behaved last night." He glanced over at Honey. "Both of you have a little understanding and give me just one more chance! The three of us have got to stick together and help each other. If we do that, we can write our own tickets on the Comstock."

The Gunsmith shifted uncomfortably in his bed. "As soon as I can, I'm ready to write a one-way ticket—the hell out of here," Clint growled. "And I think Honey is ready to join me."

"You can't do that to me!" Rick wailed. "We're

a team! We work good together and we can trust one another. I'll make us all rich in the next year.''

Rick got up and moved to Honey, his face begging for understanding. He gently placed a kiss on her forehead. ''Remember how we always make love? And how you sing to me and I keep saying that you have the voice, the face and the body to make a debut at Piper's Opera House up in Virginia City?''

Honey nodded, her eyes searched his face for some element of the truth. ''Yeah, I remember.''

''Well, I'm gonna see those people up there after we open my new saloon. You're going to have such a big following in Virginia City that the civic snobs who run that place are going to have to allow you to sing opera there.''

''But . . .''

''Listen,'' he said. ''Yesterday, I made a decision and I bought the Golden Nugget Saloon on 'C' Street.''

''The Golden Nugget!'' she whispered.

''Yeah. It needs a lot of work, and its business has sort of fallen off to the Bucket of Blood and the Delta, but we can build it back up again. The place is over three thousand square feet. It's huge and the bar and back mirror is as good as money can buy. We can make the Golden Nugget a goddamn showplace. I know that we can! Clint, if you'll handle security for me, and Honey, I promise to get you the backup of the best piano player and piano that money can buy. I'll have a stage built for you and some new costumes. We'll hire a theatrical arranger and do some real creative numbers. Do the kind of shows that they put on in San Francisco and New York. We'll make you a big name, Honey! I swear I will.''

''What about Miss Hale?'' she asked. ''What will she say to all this?''

Rick placed his hand on Honey's shoulder. "She's one part of my life that is going to have to be put on the back burner. I just don't know about her anymore. Right now, you're the one that is filling my dreams, not Miss Hale."

A tear slid down Honey's cheek and her eyes were shiny. Clint watched the stiffness drain out of her body and then saw her wrap her arms around Rick's neck and kiss him with gratitude. It was a long, passionate kiss and their lips moved hard against each other causing Clint to look away.

"Clint," Rick said, his voice hoarse with passion. "Honey and I are going to go talk over a few details and then drive up to see the Golden Nugget and decide where to build her stage and where is best to put the piano. But when I come back, I'll have some serious things to discuss."

Rick ran his hand over Honey's still undulating hips, and then he reached into the inside of his coat pocket. "Here," he said, tossing the Gunsmith a thick envelope.

"What's this for?"

"Money for the doctor, medicine, food, liquor, women. It's for whatever you want to spend it on."

"I don't need your money," Clint said abruptly.

But Rick wasn't listening. He was ushering Honey out the door and calling over his shoulder, "I'll be back this afternoon. You rest up and get to feeling better. We're going to take Virginia City starting next week!"

Before Clint could object any further, the door closed and he heard Honey giggle and then the sound of their footsteps receding down the stairs.

Hell, Clint thought. He isn't going to make Honey famous. He's just plain going to make her.

NINE

That afternoon, Clint was awakened by a knock on his door. "Who is it?"

The reply was soft, hesitant and feminine. "It's . . . it's Miss Hale."

Clint frowned and called, "I'm not fit for female company, Miss Hale."

There was a long pause, then, "Please! I saw you last night. I know what you must look like and how badly you must feel, but we have to talk."

"Damn!" Clint muttered. "Hang on while I get myself decent."

Painfully, he eased his feet out of bed and then, gritting his teeth with discomfort, he reached for his pants and pulled them on, then hobbled over to his bags where he dug out a clean shirt. He dressed slowly, studying himself in the mirror and actually wincing because he looked so bad. Damn! but those miners had worked him over bad. One eye was swollen almost shut and purplish, the left side of his face was lopsided with swelling and his front teeth were loose. He was a sorry sight indeed!

"I'm coming," he said, as he shuffled barefooted over to the door and unlocked it.

Even though she was prepared for the worst, it was obvious that Miranda Hale was shocked by his appearance. "Dear Lord!" she whispered. "You should have stayed for another cup of tea instead of heading for Rick's Saloon.''

The remark caught the Gunsmith off guard and it tickled his funnybone. ''What a silly thing to say to a man who looks like me,'' he grinned. ''But it's true. I've seen handsomer corpses.''

Miranda just managed a smile. She looked past the Gunsmith, and it was clear that she was very nervous but determined to speak with him. ''Would you close the door, please?''

''Be better for your reputation if I left it wide open.''

''I appreciate your concern, Mr. Adams, but what I have to say is too important to be overheard by some eavesdropper. I need to have some honest answers, and they are of a very personal nature.''

Clint closed the door and motioned for the young woman to take his only chair while he made his way back to the bed. Stretching out very slowly, he laced his fingers behind his head and, propped up on his pillow, he regarded the girl with a mixture of pity and dread.

''All right, Miss Hale. Why don't we get this interrogation over with. You want to know about Rick and Miss Honey, I suspect and—''

''And a whole lot more,'' she told him, her voice stretched with tension. ''You see, I am not stupid, Mr. Adams. I know that Rick has a dark side. I even . . . well, I even know that he probably owns a house of ill-repute.''

Clint's eyebrows raised. ''You know that? And you're still willing to marry him?''

She nodded. ''It would be terribly hypocritical not to. You see, my mother . . .'' Miranda had to take a deep breath before she could go on. ''My mother was a prostitute before father married her. They had to leave Colorado and went to Arizona. But someone recognized her there and so they moved again. And again. You see, a sheriff is supposed to be a paragon of virtue and no town council would permit him to marry a woman of my mother's background.''

''I was a lawman long enough to know what you say is the truth,'' Clint admitted. ''The sheriff, the banker and the parson have got to be better than God Himself. But the rest of the town can be the sinniest bunch of hypocrites you ever did see.''

''Then you understand what I am saying, Mr. Adams. And you can appreciate that whenever my mother's past was discovered my father was run out of town. It didn't matter if he'd risked his life for them, everything was forgotten the moment my mother was recognized as a former lady of the night.''

''It must have been hard on both of them,'' Clint said, generating a little more sympathy and understanding for Sheriff Hale now that he understood the man's troubled and checkered career in law.

''It was. Just when we thought we had found a new home, someone would recognize mother. It got so she never went outside, and then people thought she was crazy. Finally, in a little town in New Mexico, mother took her life, and what she left of father was less than she had found.''

Clint didn't know what to say. It was a tragic story.

Miranda touched his arm. ''I felt I had to tell you this so that you know that I am not a pillar of virtue or some naive little maiden who is going to be destroyed by the truth concerning Rick.''

Clint found his voice. ''I see. Well, since you know about the house of ill-repute, what else is there to say?''

''Maybe a lot. Maybe nothing.''

"Speak plain," Clint said. "It's clear that you have something definite to talk about."

"All right. Rick is very ambitious. I know that and even approve. But what I cannot approve and what shocked me terribly was the way that he turned on you, his best friend, last night in the street. Indeed, Mr. Adams, Rick has, for most of his adult life, placed you on a pedestal. And then, simply because you might have caused a fight that had some negative economic repercussions, the pedestal crashes and he grinds it—and you—under his heel."

Miranda stared down at her hands which were tightly clasped. "You see, Mr. Adams, for some reason, Rick also places *me* on a pedestal. And that worries me more than I can say. Especially now, when I have seen how little one can slip up and how far they can fall in his eyes. If he will turn so viciously on his best friend, he will also turn on me when I first disappoint him in marriage."

"Maybe that's not the case," Clint said, lamely. "He came here first thing this morning and apologized."

"I know he came here. I was coming here myself when I saw him enter this hotel alone, then a few minutes later I saw him and Miss Honey leave together. They didn't see me, but I saw them go only a few doors up the street and into another hotel. I even saw . . ."

Clint shook his head. "You saw too much, Miss Hale. I'm sorry."

"So am I," she whispered, her voice bitter. "He promised me that he was being true, but he lied. If I had an ounce of pride I would break the engagement, except I have very little pride left and I am deeply in love with Rick. I think I can make him into a wonderful man."

Clint looked away. Miss Honey also had that

impression. Clint had seen idealistic women attempt to be reformers hundreds of times, and the result was always the same. Women didn't change men from good to bad. Not over any length of time. Religion could change a man's heart. Tragedy sometimes brought a bad man to God and made him repent his evil ways. But women didn't do anything to a bad man but make him feel guilty. And the guiltier a bad man felt, the meaner inside he became, until he exploded in violence—often, against the decent, reform-minded woman that was the cause of his guilt.

"Miss Hale," Clint said in a gentle voice. "I'm Rick's friend but we are almost strangers. We haven't seen each other in so long we don't know how we think anymore. I don't know how to advise you except to say that you have seen that Rick is unfaithful. I don't know if he would remain unfaithful as a father and a husband, but I think you had better get accustomed to that idea if you go through with your engagement and become married. Did you know that he bought the Golden Nugget Saloon up in Virginia City?"

Her eyes widened with surprise. "Why, no!"

"Well, he did. Rick is determined to be a wealthy man. He has promised Miss Honey that he would make her famous. I leave the rest up to you."

She came to her feet, looking more confused than angry as she moved toward the door. "He had talked about it to me. But it was to be *our* decision. One we made together."

"I'm sorry," he said. "Maybe I shouldn't have told you about the purchase of the Golden Nugget, but you would have found out about it as soon as the next issue of the *Gold Hill News* was printed. I thought it better that you heard it from me rather than some stranger or from reading the paper.''

Miranda paused at the door and she looked defeated. ''I feel like I've been kicked in the face. I feel . . . I feel as bad as you look, Mr. Adams. But we'll both recover soon. Would you come to see me when that happens?''

''I don't know,'' he said.

''Would you please come to see me?''

''Why? You know what I am and have been. I'm not the kind of a man you're looking for either.''

''You presume too much,'' she said, leaving him and closing the door behind her.

Clint found that he could not get Miranda out of his thoughts during the next week while he healed and regained his mobility. Honey noticed his preoccupation, but she was so excited about the work that was being done on the Golden Nugget and the new costumes she was buying that nothing could have dampened her spirits.

As for Rick, he wore a smile on his lips, but underneath the facade, Clint could feel the man's tension. He was sure that Miranda had not spoken of her visit, but also certain that she had ended the engagement. And one afternoon as they were driving a buckboard up to Virginia with some new chairs for the Golden Nugget, Rick confirmed those suspicions.

''Miranda and I are finished,'' he said darkly. ''I finally realized that she was nothing but a millstone around my neck. She wasn't helping me to make money, and she wasn't contributing a damn thing to my confidence. I'm better off without her. What I need to find is a rich woman. One that can put me over the top.''

Clint looked sideways at his friend. ''What about

Honey? If you make her a celebrity and a big name, she'll generate all the business and money that you need.''

"Aw, she's fine. A work of art in bed, as you well remember. But she just hasn't got the class to make it big. Her voice is good, but not good enough to get her into Piper's Opera House. I know that even though she doesn't believe it. Honey is a great fuck and a first class saloon entertainer, but she's almost thirty years old and her wrinkles are starting to show.''

"I never noticed," Clint said acidly. "She's still younger than we are, and I don't feel like I'm slowing down."

Rick slapped the lines hard and the team walked faster. "Men last longer than women. A woman is in her prime and out of her prime by the time she's twenty-five. A man, hell, if he don't get himself beat up or hurt . . ." he winked at Clint . . . "then he can still go strong until he's thirty-five. I've seen a lot of miners that would rip our heads off and stuff them up our asses when they were in their fifties.''

"I don't doubt that," Clint said. "But I still think that Honey is good enough to make a big name for herself. Hell, I saw Lola Montez when she arrived in San Francisco after sailing from Europe. She'd had what . . . five or six husbands, and she was thirty-five years old. She'd lived hard but when she went on stage and did her famed Spider Dance, the men went crazy. She was a damned good looking woman at thirty-five. Better looking than most in their twenties.''

"Maybe so, but I saw Lola Montez a few years after that," Rick said. "She was already washed up and forty. And she *looked* forty. Sometimes fame can keep a woman young past her natural time. But it always catches up with them. Besides, Honey is a whore. Everybody knows that. Her past can't be ignored and the newspapers would crucify her if she ever tried to become prominent.''

Clint lapsed into silence as they drove down "C" Street, past the famous saloons and bustling businesses that were, if anything, even busier than the ones in Gold Hill. He thought about Miranda and how her own mother had also been a whore and how it had finally driven the poor creature to suicide. How come it was that a person couldn't begin each new day fresh? That he or she had to carry around the ghosts of their pasts and stumble through life trying to cover every mistake, every sin?

Clint could empathize with both Honey and Miranda's mother because his own past was often a source of danger and sadness. Danger because he still had the reputation of being one of the fastest guns alive and men were forever testing that reputation. Sadness because he had killed men that should have lived into old age but got foolish or made some deadly move that had left Clint with no choice but to shoot to kill. And some of the dead ones out of his past haunted him at night. There were occasionally nightmares. Young, dead faces whose frozen expressions were etched with shock and fatal surprise.

"I'm gonna open another brewery and whorehouse up here," Rick said later, as they unloaded the card table chairs. "By this time next year, you and I will be rolling in tall clover."

Clint said nothing. He just helped Rick unload the chairs and stack them inside the Golden Nugget Saloon. He wasn't going to be here next year. He was sure of that much. And if it hadn't been for his growing concern for Miranda and Honey, he wouldn't even have given bets that he'd be here tomorrow.

"I plan to open this place up next week. Gonna get some painters in here tomorrow and do it up real splashy." Rick pointed to a newly made stage. "That's where Honey is going to sing and dance. Her costumes are the wildest things you ever seen. You know she's got fine tits. Well, I'm gong to make sure that they're hanging out to the nipples. I'll have the customers drooling in their beer and lining out my front door."

Seeing his new saloon had greatly elevated Rick's mood, and he clapped Clint on the back. "And all *you* have to do is to keep the peace. Keep the animals off Honey and make sure they settle their debts and don't get too rowdy."

"I didn't say I'd do it," Clint told him.

Rick's smile evaporated. "You took my money, didn't you?"

"I did."

"Then you were paid for a job and you have to do it," Rick said, his voice hard-edged. "Unless you want to give the money back."

"I had to spend some of it," Clint said. "But I guess I could make up the rest easy enough if I could find an honest card game. You don't know where I could find one of those, do you?"

Rick stared at him, his eyes flashing with anger and then he burst out in laughter. "Clint, I can always count on my old blood brother to keep me honest. You're the only person I know that doesn't pull his punches or hide what he thinks."

"If I help here," he said quietly, "the games will be honest. If they're not, I'll shut you down myself. Is that understood?"

Rick's new smile died in a hurry. "Who the hell's side are you on, anyway!"

"I'm a lawman at heart," Clint replied. "Been

honest too damn long to lose my soul now over a couple hundred dollars in pay off money.''

"A couple of hundred dollars!" Rick shouted in anger. "I'm talking tens of thousand of dollars coming your way and you say a 'couple of hundred dollars!' Think big, dammit!"

Clint shook his head and walked out the door. He'd made up his mind. He was going to get Rick established out of a sense of loyalty, and then he was going to quit the Comstock before the can of worms spilled out and things got messy. He wasn't going to change Rick any more than Honey or Miss Miranda Hale.

And speaking of Miranda, he guessed he was ready to pay her a visit. He'd bought himself some new clothes, and he was ready to meet an honest person so that he could renew his faith in mankind.

TEN

Their buckboard rolled back over the divide and on down the steep, winding road toward Gold Hill. "Clint?"

The Gunsmith looked aside at Rick who had been glancing sideways at him every few minutes. "Yeah?"

"I'm glad to see that you've recovered so fast from that beating. I was really upset about that."

"I remember."

Rick frowned. "You mean about how angry I got with you?"

Clint said nothing. There were times when it was better just to let things ride and not stir up a bad memory.

"Listen," Rick said. "I told you I was sorry and I can't do anymore than that, can I?"

"Forget it," Clint said quietly.

Rick chewed on himself for a minute and then he said, "You thought any more about Bill Meeker and Jim Banks? I still think they mean to kill me. I'd like you to send them a message. If they know you're working for me, it might just scare them enough to keep them from trying anything."

Clint scowled. "You have no evidence that they pose any threat. Until then, I'm not even sure what I could even talk to them about."

"You can warn them," Rick said, heat creeping

into his voice. "All I'm asking is that you go to their saloon and let it be known that the Gunsmith is standing at my side. That isn't much to ask."

Clint expelled a deep breath. "All right," he said. "I'll go have a talk with them this afternoon. I'll tell them that you had better not catch a stray bullet. Will that satisfy you?"

"Damn right," Rick said. "That's what I wanted you to do in the first place."

"Funny," Clint drawled. "Seems to me you wanted me to kill them outright when their names were first mentioned."

"That'd be murder," Rick groused. "If I said that, I was just blowin' smoke. I sure didn't think you'd take me serious."

"Rick, I take you almost as seriously as you take yourself."

Rick's face turned red with anger and the muscles in his cheeks stood out as if his flesh was stretched over wire. "You know something? I don't think you and I are gonna work out over the long run if you don't change your attitude about me and the way I view things. I asked you to come here because I thought we could help each other. But you seem more interested in Honey and Miranda and my personal life than how I intend to make us both wealthy men."

"A man's personal life *is* his life!" Clint snapped. "And from what I'm learning, your life has turned a whole lot for the worse since we were kids. I can admire ambition. I wish I had more of it myself, but I don't. What bothers me is the way you treat people."

"Like Miranda and Honey?"

"Yeah. And I'm also pretty interested in what happened to your ex-partner, Dave Fartley."

Rick had been about to say something, but at the

mention of Fartley's name, his mouth crimped down at the corners and he lashed the team.

"Well?" Clint demanded.

"What do you want to know! The son of a bitch ran out on me when we were ten thousand dollars in debt and he took every dime we had in the safe. I was almost lynched by some of my creditors before I could make things right. But I eventually did. That bastard is probably on the French Riviera living the good life while I'm here busting my tail and humping from sunup to sundown just to make ends meet."

Clint snorted with ill-concealed mirth. "Come on, Rick! You never busted your tail in your life. You told me all you've ever done is gamble. I doubt you've ever done a real day's work. Hauling those chairs up to the Golden Nugget was probably the hardest thing you've done since you can remember. And any man who owns a whorehouse, a brewery and two saloons can't expect anyone to believe him when he starts crying poor mouth."

Rick could not stay mad and, in fact, he even chuckled at himself. "Yeah, I guess coming from a man who hasn't much more than a horse, a gun and a used up sheriff's badge, I look as if I'm doing pretty fine. Well, maybe I am. But that doesn't mean I can't do a whole lot better. And I'd like to help you do a lot better too."

Clint shifted on the buckboard seat. "Rick, I'm a reasonably happy man who likes to be around happy people. So don't trouble yourself none about making me rich. If rich is something you've got to be, then that's your business. All I want is to grow old and to have a few good friends and a good woman."

"You could marry Miranda," he clipped. "She was all ready to marry me. Maybe it's just meant to be that you stepped into the breach and took my place. Her father is a sheriff so she must have a high opinion of lawmen."

"Don't put crazy ideas into my head," Clint said. "You're a wealthy man, I'm a poor one. Sometimes, it's all I can do is feed myself and my horse."

"I said I could change that for good," Rick argued.

Clint looked closely at his friend. "Okay," he said. "If it's all the same to you, I think I will pay a visit to Miss Hale."

It wasn't all right with Rick. Clint saw his cheeks flush with jealous anger but the fool had too much pride to say anything except, "Then do it!"

"I will," the Gunsmith grunted. "Soon as we unhitch the team."

Miranda Hale saw the Gunsmith coming up the hill toward her house at just about sundown. She smiled and walked out onto her porch. "You're too late for supper, but I do have some apple pie left over from dessert."

"Sounds good to me," Clint said, coming through the gate and up the porch stairs.

"The sheriff is inside," Miranda said. "He's quite a fan of yours, you know. Why don't you come inside and say hello."

Clint stepped inside, removing his hat. Sheriff Hale was sitting at the dining room table reading a copy of the *Gold Hill News*, but when he saw the Gunsmith, he dropped the paper and beamed. "Why, what an honor it is to see you, Gunsmith!"

"Clint. I'd sure appreciate it if you'd just call me by my given name, Sheriff."

Hale nodded. "All right, but if I was young and famous, I'd rather have people know me as the Gunsmith."

Miranda scoffed. "Clint is modest, father. Modesty is something that you've never quite cultivated."

"Hush now!" the man said with mock anger. "A sheriff deserves more respect. Clint, you ought to have some of that apple pie that Miranda baked. She's a pretty fair cook. Rick says there is none better."

Clint glanced at Miranda and decided that she had not told her father that her engagement with Rick Hadley had been broken. It surprised him. On the surface, at least, Miranda and her father appeared very close.

"Clint, I been meaning to ask you if you ever saw John Wesley Hardin draw his gun."

"No," Clint said. "I never did. But I understand he was fast and a dead shot."

"Would you say your big advantage is speed, or accuracy?"

Clint shrugged. "I'd say that I probably have both. You have to have both to survive the gunfights that I've been forced to take part in. That, and a lot of luck."

"That's a fact," Hale said. "Sometimes luck is the most important thing of all. Why, I remember a time down in Bisbee, Arizona, when . . ."

"Sheriff!" a cry sounded from out in the street. "You better come running! Someone tried to ambush Rick Hadley outside his saloon."

Miranda dropped the dish of pie she had been about to serve the Gunsmith, but Clint didn't notice. He was out of the dining room and bolting through the door with Sheriff Hale puffing along behind.

"Is he dead!" Clint yelled.

The man who had arrived with the news was out of breath from running uphill. "No!" he shouted, as

Miranda passed him and gained on her own father.
"But he's been hit!"

Clint was the first one to round the corner and
charge into the big knot of people who surrounded
Rick who was on his feet and holding his arm, while
the doctor inspected what appeared to be little more
than a flesh wound. Rick's starched white shirt was
ruined, the sleeve soaked with blood.

Clint reached his side and said, "What happened!"

Rick waited until the doctor had finished his work,
and then he said, "I'm all right. We need to talk in
private."

At just that moment, Miranda arrived. She squirmed
through the crowd and when she saw Rick she exclaimed, "Thank God that you're alive!"

He smiled at her and arched his eyebrows. "You
mean it still matters?"

Miranda hugged his neck. "Of course it does!"

Rick kissed her and squeezed her tight. Clint noticed that his gunshot wound didn't seem to bother
him at all. Rick threw back his head, howled at the
stars, then swung Miranda completely around in a
circle and yelled, "Listen up everybody. It looks
like me and Miss Hale are back together again. So
it's drinks on the house!"

The crowd surged into the saloon and left Rick,
Miranda and the Gunsmith standing outside with the
doctor and a very out-of-breath sheriff who managed
to gasp, "We better go to my office and make out a
report, Rick."

"The hell with that," Rick said. "I saw the man
that shot me. It was Bill Meeker."

"Are you sure?" Clint asked, watching the doctor
snap his medical kit shut.

"Yeah. He was across the street in the alley between those two stores. He stepped out, took a bead on me and opened fire.''

"Any witnesses?"

"Sure there are!" Rick said. "Sheriff, I want Meeker arrested for attempted murder.''

Sheriff Hale swallowed loudly then rubbed his jowls. "I don't know, Mr. Hadley," he weedled. "I should have a witness or two before . . .''

Rick's face grew ugly. "Sheriff, if you want to wear that badge even one more day, then you had better arrest Meeker before I send the Gunsmith along to do it.''

Miranda paled. "But Rick! You know Bill Meeker. While I suppose he might come in peacefully, if Jim Banks gets wind of an arrest, there is sure to be trouble.''

Rick glanced at Clint. "You gonna back him up, or what?''

"I'll back him up," Clint said, turning away from the couple and starting up the street in step with the sheriff.

When they reached the Sawdust Saloon, they hesitated for a minute outside the doors. "Tell me what I should expect," the Gunsmith said. "Is this Meeker a hotheaded fool that's going to sling lead the minute he understands that he's being arrested?''

"He's generally a reasonable man," the sheriff said. "It's his partner that is the hotheaded one. Jim Banks is a real tall, skinny fella, but he's awfully quick with a gun or a knife.''

"Just so I recognize him, how tall?''

" 'Bout six and a half feet. He wears a suit and a bow tie. Hair is stringy and long on the sides and all gone on the top. You can't mistake Jim for anyone you ever seen before. Me and Jim has had a couple of nasty run-ins. I consider him as deadly as a

rattlesnake. He and I both know he could probably
fill his hand and empty his gun into me before I
could clear leather.''

"Then maybe I ought to go in and bring Meeker
out by myself. I can most likely catch him completely off guard.''

"There's truth in that,'' Hale said, unable to hide
his relief. "I guess it would be the best thing all the
way around if I waited out here.''

Clint left the man quickly. Since Miranda had told
him about her father's miserable years of trying to
live with his wife's past, Clint had mustered up a
little sympathy. But still, Hale had no business being
a lawman and while he probably wasn't a coward,
he sure didn't seem much inclined to perform his
duties.

"All right,'' Clint said. "When I go in, you
station yourself just outside the door where you can
hear what's going on. If there's trouble, you'd damn
sure better draw your gun and come in for the dance.
If you hang back, I'll take it real unkindly.''

"I'll back you up,'' Hale promised.

The interior of the Sawdust Saloon was modest
when compared to Rick's thriving establishment. There
were about thirty miners at the bar and six or seven
poker games in progress toward the back of the
room. But it was easy to see that the owners, Bill
Meeker and Jim Banks, sure weren't making a bun-
dle of money.

When he approached the bar, a short, round man
with a bald head and pudgy cheeks was pouring
drinks. The man grinned and said, "What'll it be,
Mister?''

"A whiskey and I'd like you to point me out a
fella named Bill Meeker.''

The bartender's smile broadened. "Why, I'm

Meeker. What can I do for you besides slake your thirst?''

Clint blinked with surprise. ''You're Bill Meeker?''

''That's right. Anything wrong?''

Clint downed his whiskey. ''Mr. Meeker, Sheriff Hale is outside and he wants to speak with you right now.''

Meeker's smile fizzled. ''What does that worthless son of a bitch want with me?''

''A few answers. Why don't you come on out?''

''Who the hell are you, a new deputy or somethin'?''

''Yeah,'' Clint said, aware that all conversation in the room had died. ''Come on outside.''

Meeker glanced across the room toward a table of card players toward a tall, thin fellow wearing a black frock coat, red bow tie and starched white shirt. ''Any trouble, Bill?''

''Sheriff Hale wants to see me outside.''

''Who is this fella?''

Meeker looked to the Gunsmith. ''I dunno.''

The tall man pushed back his chair and then he eased back his coat so that the butt of his gun was handy to grab. He was in his late thirties and as he came closer, Clint guessed he had once been a professional gunfighter. He just had the look in his eye of a man who knew what he was doing and possessed all the confidence in the world.

Bill stopped and said, ''I don't want no trouble in here. But you can tell that fat maggot who calls himself a sheriff to come in here if he wants to talk. Tell him we know he's on Rick Hadley's payroll and that he's a disgrace to the badge he wears. Tell him we'll talk to him anyway 'cause we are law-abidin' citizens. But it has to be in here, not out in the street.''

Clint expelled a deep breath. It was never a good

idea to confront someone in their own house or place of work because they had the advantage of familiarity. And yet, it was better to bring the sheriff inside than it was to start a bunch of trouble that might be avoidable.

"Sheriff! Come on in here."

A moment later, the sheriff pushed through the door. His shirttail was hanging out and would prevent him from making a good play for his gun and his belly protruded over his belt. He looked like a whipped dog that would come slinking into a room expecting another beating. He'd even forgotten his badge again, and he was a sorry excuse for a lawman. Clint figured that if there was trouble he had better try and take Jim Banks out of the play quick and then dive for cover because the sheriff wasn't going to be any help at all.

The sheriff nodded to the two saloon owners. "Howdy," he said. "I guess the Gunsmith told you I have to ask a few questions of you, Mr. Meeker."

At the mention of his name, Jim Banks blinked. "*You're* the Gunsmith?"

"I been called that in some places," Clint said quietly. He wondered what would happen now. Knowing that they were facing the Gunsmith usually took the belligerence out of most people, but it made a few reckless and daring.

The tall man pulled his hands away from his sides. "I don't want to draw on you, Gunsmith, but if you try to jail my partner, then you better have a damn good reason. We got at least a dozen good friends in this room and they won't let Bill get stampeded into no jail."

Clint waited for the sheriff to explain things, but when the explanation was too slow in coming, he stated the facts himself. "Rick Hadley says that Bill shot him in the arm a few minutes ago. He says that he saw him plainly.''

"He's lying!'' Meeker cried. "I been tending bar since early this afternoon. You can ask anyone in the place!''

Clint looked around the room. Men were nodding their heads. One called. "We been drinking since noon and Bill has been pouring almost since the start. Every man in here will swear to that.''

Jim Banks nodded. "So what's your next move, Gunsmith? Are you going to believe a cheat and a low-down son of a bitch like Hadley, or are you going to believe the whole bunch of us?''

Clint knew that he should have said something to the tall saloon owner about calling his friend a son of a bitch, but it seemed appropriate given the fact that Clint believed these men were telling the truth.

"Sheriff, I think'' Clint said, "that we had better have another talk with Rick.''

"Well somebody shot him!''

"Yeah,'' Clint said. "But it wasn't either one of these men. So let's get out of here.''

The tall man grinned. "Most men as fast as you're supposed to be are bullies. I'm glad to see that you aren't on the same payroll as your fat friend here.''

The sheriff blustered. "I won't stand for that kind of insult.''

"Oh yes you will, you overstuffed lard ass. Now get back to your boss and kiss his behind and let us go back to the business of running a saloon.''

The sheriff tried to work up a reply, but it was so pathetic an effort that he just turned on his heel and stomped out the door without a word. Clint shook his head with disgust and went after him.

"Gunsmith!''

Clint spun and his hand flashed for his gun. It

came up in a blur and it was leveled right at Jim Banks whose own hands were resting on the bar. Banks grinned. "My, my," he whispered, "that was a thing of beauty to behold."

Clint cussed silently. "It could have gotten you killed!"

"Yeah, reckon it could have from anyone less than a real professional," Banks said. "But it was worth the risk to see how fast you really are."

"You want to test me again?" Clint challenged, mad clear through.

"Hell no," Banks swore. "Not on my best day. You leave that paid puppet and come back for a drink or two with us—on the house."

Clint relaxed and holstered his gun. "I might just do that," he said as he turned and walked toward the door. "But first, Rick had damn sure better have some good answers to my next questions."

ELEVEN

Sheriff Hale had to struggle to catch up with the Gunsmith and it left him out of breath. "Clint!" he wheezed. "Whoa up there a minute!"

The Gunsmith did not slow down at all. "What do you want?"

"I think we had better just settle down and talk this thing over a couple of minutes before you go barging into Rick's Saloon and causing a ruckus."

"There's a time for talking and a time for doing. This is the latter."

"Maybe you're wrong!" Hale shouted.

"And maybe you ought to leave me alone and go find a safe hole to crawl into!"

"Yeah," Hale said. "Well I guess you don't remember how you got beat up the last time you went in there lookin' for trouble? Might be that this time would be even worse."

Clint slammed on the brakes and spun around to glare at the red-faced, overweight and underworked man. "What kind of a sheriff are you!" he demanded. "You don't wear your badge, you're on Rick's payroll and you haven't the guts to come in and stop a fight."

To Clint's surprise, Hale grabbed his arm and spun him around. "Let me tell you something! I was sheriffin' and stopping fights when you were still runnin' around in diapers. I was a damn good sheriff, too!''

"Well, that may be true, but you aren't anymore," Clint said. "And a man like you is going to get himself backed into a corner sooner or later and then you'll have to decide either to run or fight. And if you run, you're going to embarrass your daughter and yourself so bad that you'll never live your shame down. You ought to hand in your badge."

"I lost the damn thing! And if you think you can do such a hot job, then you can find the son of a bitch, pin it to your heart and let the drunks in Gold Hill use it for target practice!"

Clint scowled. "Are you serious about quitting the law?"

"Sure I am! Nobody else wants the damn job. It don't pay but fifty dollars a month, and a man can make damn near that much in the mines. The mines ain't near as dangerous as wearing the sheriff's badge."

"What are you going to do for a living if I take the job until this is over?"

"I don't know," Hale admitted, suddenly looking very old and defeated. "I ain't got no money saved up or nothin'. I was hoping that my daughter would get married and then I'd only have myself to worry about."

"Your daughter is old enough to support herself," Clint said. "And I suspect that she's plenty capable of doing it."

"Yeah, as a matter of fact, she is," Hale said as they trudged up the boardwalk. "But I didn't think it'd look right for her to be workin'."

"You have some strange ideas," Clint said. "The best thing for Miranda would be to find a job and start making enough money so that you could retire.

You may have been a good sheriff once upon a time, but time has caught up with you and you're a man that's flirtin' with an early grave.''

The sheriff puffed along beside the Gunsmith for another block, and then he seemed to make up his mind. ''Okay, then that's what I'm going to do. You're the sheriff. Here are the keys to the office and the rifle rack.''

''Those rifles are history,'' Clint said, taking the keys. ''I sure wouldn't put my life on the line with one of them antiques.''

''I forgot that you really are a gunsmith,'' the ex-sheriff said. ''Yeah, I inherited that bunch and they aren't much. None of them shoots straight. Couple look as if they are ready to explode.''

''That jail cell doesn't look too good either,'' Clint said. ''You ever have any prisoners?''

''No,'' Hale said. ''The city won't pay but two bits a day for feedin' 'em and I can't do it for that. I'd have to dig into my own pocket, and I don't make enough money to be that charitable.''

''I need to talk to the town council or whoever has the last say on all this,'' Clint grumbled.

''There ain't no town council,'' Hale groused. ''That's half the problem.''

''Then who pays your wages?''

''You named him,'' Hale said. ''Along with a couple other of the most successful businessmen.''

''You mean you have no payroll? You're reduced to the charity of the saloon owners and a few other businessmen?''

Hale nodded. ''Pretty pitiful, ain't it.''

''It sure as hell is,'' Clint said. ''No wonder you haven't exactly been bustin' your butt to clean up things in Gold Hill.''

''I better tell you something before you go into

Rick's Saloon. He's the main man that is behind what the sheriff gets or doesn't get in the way of a salary. He'll swing a few dollars extra your way if you play his game."

"Not a chance," Clint said. "I'm afraid I damn near played his game when I went into the Sawdust Saloon figuring to arrest Bill Meeker. I got a feeling that Rick set me up to kill an innocent man."

"Rick can be sort of ruthless when he wants to be," Hale admitted. "But you have to admire the way he's made something of himself in these parts. That's why I didn't say anything about Miranda marrying a man like that. She's got a soft heart and I was always afraid that she'd fall in love with some poor, broke miner who'd get her with a couple of children and then get himself snuffed out in a mine cave-in. Then where would she be? Poor and in a bad fix with an old man like me to worry about on top of all her other problems."

"Miranda has more steel in her backbone than you think," Clint said, as they neared Rick's Saloon. "Why do you figure Rick is so set on getting Meeker and Banks out of the way?"

"He wants their saloon," Hale said. "In case you didn't notice, they got the finest chandeliers and back bar mirror on the Comstock. That bar is imported from France. Rick has seen 'em and offered both men a lot of money but they refuse to sell out."

"And that's it?"

"Not quite. You see, Miss Honey was once Jim Banks's woman. He was good to her, and she worked in the Sawdust Saloon until Rick charmed and then hired her away. Jim Banks went and challenged Rick to a gunfight with fifty or sixty men watching. Rick backed down 'cause he knew that Banks was fast. I think it shamed Rick so bad he's never forgot how

Banks laughed at him. He hates Jim Banks worse than anything. And little Bill Meeker is always making jokes about Rick. He's got a way of mimicking him that's mighty funny.''

"I see," Clint said, thinking about how much pride Rick had and how such actions would be viewed. "That pretty well explains everything."

Hale stopped outside the saloon. "I don't guess I need to go in there with you. After all, I told you I was quitting."

"No," Clint said. "You can go home. Think of something safer to do than being a lawman."

"But it's all I ever did for a living."

Clint said, "People are always having to make changes. Every cowboy I ever knew had to hang up his chaps and spurs sooner or later. They become cooks or whatever. Nobody who isn't afraid of a little work ever seems to starve in these towns. I'm sure if you give it some real thought, you can find a way to make a living here."

Hale started looking hopeful. "You know, you're a pretty nice fella, Clint. I guess I been hanging onto something I should have let go of a long time ago."

"That happens." Clint stuck out his hand. "Go home and relax. I'll be talking to you in the days to come."

"If you kill Rick, I don't think they'll let you stay sheriff in this town," Hale said quietly.

"I'm not going to kill him. We're friends."

"Even after what he did?"

"Yes, if he still wants to be."

"Who do you think shot Rick, if it wasn't Meeker?"

"I don't know," Clint admitted. "That's the big question. I think I might know the answer but I'll just have to wait and see."

Clint could tell that Hale wanted to hear his theory, but the Gunsmith figured he'd said enough as he pushed into the saloon. Since Miss Honey had quit singing here, the crowd had thinned out considerably and he had no trouble going to Rick's corner. As always, the three bouncers looked as if they wanted to challenge him, but Clint just shouldered past them and took a seat beside Rick.

"Well," Rick said, "tell me what happened. Did you have to shoot them both, or just Jim Banks?"

"I didn't shoot either one," he said as he called for a beer. "Meeker isn't the man that wounded you."

Even in the dimness, Clint could see Rick stiffen with anger. "What the hell do you mean? I saw him myself!"

"Meeker has a saloon full of witnesses that say he hasn't left the bar all afternoon."

"They're lying!"

"Uhn-uh," Clint said. "Fifty men can't lie that good. Who really shot you, Rick? Or did you just cut yourself with a knife and fire your own gun into the sky?"

Rick exploded with outrage. "What the hell are you talking about! Whose side are you on!"

In answer, Clint grabbed the man's sleeve and yanked both the coat and shirt sleeve up so that the bandage was exposed. In the same motion, he drew his gun and pointed it at Rick saying, "You tell your gorillas to stay put or I'll pistol-whip you hard enough to send you to sleep for a long time."

The bouncers had turned at the sound of Rick's angry voice and when they saw the gun in Clint's hands, they went for their own guns.

"No!" Rick cried. "Put your guns away, you fools!"

The men did as they were told.

Clint relaxed. "Tell them to go have a drink while we talk."

"Go have a drink," Rick said in a voice that trembled with anger. "I'll be all right."

When the bouncers had gone, Clint laid his gun down on the table before them and said, "Take off the bandage and let me see that flesh wound."

"What are you trying to prove!"

"You know the answer to that as well as I do," Clint said. "Now take it off!"

Rick had no choice but to obey him. He pulled the bandage off and Clint stared at the fresh wound. "Knife wound," he said with disgust. "You cut yourself and made it all up to look as if you were ambushed."

"You're crazy!"

Clint pushed away just as his beer came. He holstered his gun, stood and then downed the beer. "We're finished," he said. "You tried to get me to shoot an innocent pair of men so that you could take over their saloon. I'm sure it occurred to you that I might also be killed but that didn't stop you from going through with your miserable little plot."

"Get out of here," Rick said. "From this day, this hour, minute forth, we are no longer blood brothers but enemies."

"Are you sure that's the way it's going to be?"

"It is," Rick choked.

"Then I should tell you one last thing. Sheriff Hale has resigned and given me his badge and keys. I'm going to clean up things around Gold Hill. I'll do it before I leave and you're one of the first orders of my new business."

"You can't just appoint yourself sheriff!"

"I didn't appoint myself, Sheriff Hale appointed

me. And by the time you manage to get me fired, I'll have you either running an honest saloon and minding your own business, or in my jail.''

Rick had a bottle of whiskey and when he poured a drink, his hand was shaking so badly that the neck of the bottle rattled on the edge of his glass. ''If you don't get on your horse and ride off the Comstock, I'm going to have to do something serious and permanent about you.''

But Clint wasn't listening as he spun on his heel and walked out the door. He felt sick about having his old best friend suddenly become his newest and worst enemy. However, that was life. Rick had dealt him into this game and if he just walked away from it, he'd always feel ashamed that he'd left a town at the mercy of a man who had gone bad.

And while he was thinking about it, he guessed that in addition to saving the town, he might as well try and talk some sense into Miss Hale and Miss Honey. Sure, they were as different as day and night, but they were both good women under Rick's bad spell.

It was a spell that was going to be tough to break.

TWELVE

"What's wrong?" Clint asked, the moment he walked into the hotel and saw a small crowd gathered at the foot of the stairs listening to a loud argument on the second floor.

The hotel desk clerk turned quickly. "I think Rick is going to murder Miss Honey," he said. "They been arguing for almost two hours. I heard the sound of his hand on her and then she cried out."

Clint surged forward. He shoved people aside and when he gained the stairs, he took them two at a time. His gun was in his fist when he reached the top of the landing and the voices were loud and angry.

'Goddamn you!" Honey cried. "You had him shot! Admit it!"

"You're crazy!" Rick shouted. "And if you don't shut up, I'll cave your damned face in!"

"I hate you, Rick!"

Clint heard the sound of flesh striking flesh again and when he slammed through the door and leveled his gun at Rick, the man was standing over Miss Honey. His fists were doubled up and the woman was on the floor.

Clint cocked his six-gun, and at the sound of it Rick spun around, his own hand going for his pistol.

"Don't!" Clint ordered in a low voice that seemed loud.

Rick froze. His fingers twitched over his gun butt. "You don't want to be here, Clint. So just put that gun away and back on out. This is between her and me."

"Not anymore it isn't," the Gunsmith said.

Honey looked up. The right side of her face was bruised and there were purplish finger marks on her neck. It was a wonder that Rick hadn't strangled her because it was obvious that he had tried.

"You're under arrest," Clint said.

"You're crazy!"

Clint did not blink nor did his grim expression change. "If I hadn't walked in here you might have beaten her to death. I'm charging you with assault and battery. You can do your explaining to a judge."

"There ain't no damn judge on the Comstock!" Rick hissed.

"Then we'll go to Carson City," Clint said stubbornly. "Just as soon as I get a wagon full of prisoners. Now unbuckle the gun."

Honey picked herself up. "Let him go," she said, her voice soft and pleading. "This will come to no good. I'll say that . . . that I walked into a wall. I won't press charges, Clint."

The Gunsmith swore silently. "Why not!"

"I . . . I just won't." She stumbled over to a wash bowl and dipped a cloth into it and then began to sponge her face and neck.

"Well?" Rick demanded. "What the hell are you going to do? The woman said that she wouldn't press charges. You can't arrest me for yelling at her."

Clint looked at Honey. She was avoiding his eyes, and he knew that he was licked. "I heard her say that you had someone killed. Who was it?"

"I had nobody killed!" Rick spat. "She's crazy as a damn loon."

Honey's head jerked up. "I can't prove it, Clint. But Jim Banks was gunned down this morning as he was opening up the Sawdust Saloon. Someone shot him from ambush."

Rick smiled grimly. "Jim Banks was a vicious killer. A gunfighter like yourself. A man who gloried in putting fear into others. He had many enemies. I was just one of them."

"You wanted me to kill him," Clint said. "When you cut your own arm and sent me to the Sawdust Saloon to arrest Bill Meeker, you were counting on Jim Banks to step in and save his friend. You expected us to go for our guns and for me to beat him. When that didn't work out as planned, you had one of your men—probably the one named Frankie—ambush him."

"That's smoke and bullshit," Rick snorted. "You haven't a thread of evidence to go on and neither does Honey. I fired you and now you both want my balls hanging on your war lances—but for different reasons. You can go fuck yourselves to death for all I care."

Clint stared at the man that he had once thought of as his blood brother. Rick Hadley had become a stranger as well as a very dangerous enemy. "All right," he said. "Get out of here."

Rick chuckled out loud. He was not quite finished. "You're both a couple of losers. I could have made you each a lot of money. Instead, you chose to turn on me and you'll get nothing in this town. No fame for you, Honey. You haven't got the talent to sing opera in a flop house. And you, Clint, you—"

Whatever he was about to say ended very abruptly when Clint took three quick steps forward and hooked a wicked uppercut to Rick's handsome jaw. The saloon owner reeled backward into the hall and crashed into the far wall before he slumped to the floor.

Holding his jaw, he looked up at the Gunsmith and said, "You got twenty-four hours to get off the Comstock Lode, and then you are the same as a dead man."

Clint's eyebrows arched. "Tell me this. Are you going to do the fighting or are you going to have one of your hired gorillas back shoot me?"

"You'll never know," Rick choked. "You'll just be dead."

Clint stepped back into Honey's room and slammed the door shut. He walked over to where she kept a bottle of whiskey, and he poured two glasses half full. Handing one to Honey, he took the other and studied its amber liquid for a moment before he said, "Good riddance to bad rubbish."

"He ain't rubbish, that one," Honey said thickly. "He's poison is what he is. And if we were smart, we'd clear off the Comstock and be done with all this."

Clint drank deeply. The whiskey cleared his head rather than clouded it. "I've never been too smart when it came to someone who threatened to kill me. I've always sort of went right at the person until they either had a change of heart or I killed them."

Honey sniffled. "You didn't know Jim Banks, did you?"

"I just met him the other evening in his saloon. I had the feeling he was a bold man. A former gunfighter."

"You pegged him right," she said, still dabbing at her bruises with the damp washcloth. "I first met him in Abilene. We were real young then. I was just sixteen, he was two years older. He was as wild as a tornado and as handsome as the devil. I loved him enough to follow him from town to town for almost five years."

"What happened to stop you from doing it longer?"

"Jim shot a man by mistake. He was an innocent bystander. A farmer with a family. He had three kids and when he died he left them nothing but debts. Jim Banks never hired out his gun again. He sent money to the wife and the kids for many years even though they cursed his name. That was the kind of a man he was after you got under that tough exterior he had for show."

The Gunsmith walked over to her and touched her cheek. "I'm sorry Banks died in an ambush. I'll go over and investigate. I'm the new Gold Hill sheriff."

"You're a dead man and you'll find no clues. Rick is too smart to do something like that himself. You'll never make the connection."

"Probably not," Clint agreed. "But I still have to try. Sometimes, you get lucky. Maybe someone saw it happen. Maybe there is a witness or perhaps the man that Rick hired will start bragging and I'll hear a rumor and learn his identity. If I can do that much, then I have something to work toward."

"But what if you get absolutely nothing?" Honey asked in a dull voice. "What if no one says a damn thing and all you can do is to walk away?"

"Then I'll walk," Clint said. "I've done it many times before."

"So that means that Rick will get off free."

Clint kissed her cheeks. "This time, maybe. But after twenty-four hours have passed, he'll send a man after me. If I'm good and a little bit lucky, I'll stop that man without killing him. He'll talk, and then I'll have enough evidence to arrest Rick Hadley for attempted murder. He'll go to prison."

Honey turned and studied her face in the mirror, then shook her head. "I look old tonight," she said. "Old and battered."

"You were battered," the Gunsmith said, reaching for her, then turning her around and pulling her to his chest. "Maybe you need to be held awhile."

"I really do if you've got the time," she said, her voice small and defeated.

Clint walked over to the door and then locked it before he went to the bed and began to undress. Honey watched him strip down to nothing, and then she made herself smile. "You have more scars on your body than any man I ever saw."

"I've led a hard life," he told her, with the beginning of a grin tugging up the corners of his lips. "But I have had my moments."

Honey nodded and undressed. She practically rushed across the room and threw herself into his arms as they tumbled onto the bed. "Screw me until I sing again," she begged.

Clint was more than happy to oblige. He wanted to momentarily erase the thought of Rick, and how they had both expected a friendship to pick up where it had left off twenty some years before. He rolled Honey over onto her stomach and spread her legs apart, then entered her from behind. She groaned with pleasure as he moved hard in and out of her womanhood.

"I want to see you do it," she whispered. "Let me up a little."

Clint slipped back out of her, and the woman lifted to her hands and knees. "Now," she said, hanging her head down and reaching under her body to guide his stiff manhood back inside of her.

Clint drove his hips hard against her buttocks, his stiff rod pumping with a strong rhythm. One of his hands reached for her breast, and she moaned with pleasure as he rolled her nipple between his thumb and forefinger. He knew she was watching the union of their bodies and that the view was exciting her greatly. She was wagging her behind like the tail of a dog and it felt wonderful to them both.

"Don't stop," she panted.

Clint had no intention of stopping. He kept driving into her until she was right up against the wall. Once, when he started to back away to give her some head room, she protested with a whimper so he just let her bump against the wall until they both lost control and started making a lot of noise.

Afterward, they lay wrapped up together, calm and contented. Hours passed without breaking a silence until Honey said, "Clint?"

"Yeah?"

"You'll have to kill him. He won't stop now that he's given you a death sentence. He'll find a way to put a bullet into you."

"No he won't," the Gunsmith said. "I'll kill him first, if I have to."

"What about Miss Hale?"

Clint raised up and looked down at her. "What about Miss Hale?"

"Well, I thought that she ought to know about what kind of a man Rick Hadley really is."

"I think she already knows," Clint said. "Maybe she doesn't care."

"She'll care the first time he beats her," Honey vowed.

Clint said nothing because he supposed that Honey was right. Miranda Hale would not take a beating and no matter how much in love with Rick she thought she was, she'd leave him in a minute if it could be proved that Rick was a murderer. Maybe that was the only way she would face the truth.

THIRTEEN

Clint stood beside the somber little mortician as they both stared at the body of Jim Banks. A rifle bullet had struck Jim squarely in the chest and there was no doubt that the man had died instantly.

"I never liked him," the mortician said. "But I'm Christian enough to say that I'm glad he didn't suffer and that the bullet didn't ruin his homely face."

The mortician's hands fluttered over the body in anticipation of the work he would soon be doing. The man wore glasses and had big bags under his eyes. He was pale and his teeth were badly stained by tobacco. He smelled like formaldehyde, there was a layer of dandruff as thick as snow on the heavily padded shoulders of his black coat, and he gave Clint the creeps.

"He never knew what hit him," Clint said. "I'm surprised that the bullet didn't come out his back."

The mortician dipped his head and pulled his delicate hands back to clasp them over his dirty vest. "If the bullet would have hit him in the face, it'd a blown the back of his skull along with his brains all over that alley. I seen it before. Makes a terrible mess!"

He touched his brow like a woman about to faint. "Honestly, Mr. Adams. I just hate it when that happens."

Clint eased away from the man a little more. "You hear anyone say they were there when he was shot?"

"Well, I just don't think anyone would have been up at that hour. Six o'clock may be sleeping in for the miners, but for us city folks, it's much too early to be up and about. Even the drunks are passed out under the boardwalk or over at the stables in a hay pile."

"There might have been someone," Clint persisted. He pulled a couple of rumpled greenbacks from his pockets and said, "If you hear of anything, there's more where this came from."

The mortician was not impressed, but he took the money anyway. "Two dollars? Big deal."

Clint almost lost his temper. "Listen, it is a big deal! I'm the new sheriff, and I intend to find out who did this and then send them either to the gallows or to prison. I also aim to clean up Gold Hill and make it respectable."

"Who appointed you sheriff?"

"The last man who had the job," Clint said, striding toward the door. "And since there's no town council to vote me a pay raise with the job. I'll be coming around in a week or so to collect my dues."

The mortician glared at him before he straightened to his full height which was not one bit impressive. "I can't speak for the other professional businessmen of Gold Hill, but for myself, I'll pay you exactly nothing, Mr. Adams."

"Then you'll be your own last customer," Clint said over his shoulder. "You had better think hard about that."

He slammed the door and went back once again to the Sawdust Saloon where Jim Banks had fallen.

He'd already spent nearly an hour there but it was his belief that, when a lawman had nothing to go on, it was better to keep going over the scene of the crime rather than sitting on his thumbs all locked up with worry.

Clint went over every inch of the scene but again found nothing. The problem was, there were footprints everywhere because at least a dozen curious townspeople had come and walked all over the place erasing any possible leads. Clint did not even have a clue as to where the hidden assassin had fired from. Across the street, certainly, but it could have been from any number of places.

"Mister?"

Clint turned to see a boy of about twelve. He was round-cheeked, with large blue eyes, brown hair and buckteeth. He looked nervous and was cracking the knuckles of his right hand. "You the Gunsmith?" he asked in a high voice.

"I am."

"You gonna be the new sheriff?"

"I am," Clint repeated.

"I saw Mr. Banks fall," the boy said, looking over his shoulder as if he were afraid they were being watched. "I saw it all."

Clint blinked, then nodded. He had been a lawman too many years to allow himself to get unduly excited or optimistic. More than one boy this age had strung out some big lie just to get his attention. "Keep talking."

"Mr. Banks was fumbling for his keys to that lock on the door. He was havin' the same trouble he did every morning."

"Are you here every morning?" Clint asked.

"Except Sunday. You see, I deliver a quart of milk every single day."

"To the Sawdust Saloon?" Clint's voice betrayed his skepticism.

"Oh, yes sir! You see, Mr. Banks, he had an ulcer. You can ask Doc Peoples about it and he'll tell you that he told Mr. Banks to drink milk first thing in the morning."

"Then why didn't he just go to a café?"

The boy shrugged. "He thought it would look funny, him owning a saloon and drinking milk. And that's the God's honest truth."

Clint believed the boy. The story was too ridiculous to be fable. "All right. So you deliver milk to him every morning and you saw him when he fell. Did you also see who shot him?"

"Yes, sir . . . well, not exactly. I saw him moving in the shadows across the street. I saw him kinda twist around real sudden like when Mr. Banks drew his gun and shot him."

"Now wait a minute!" Clint said. "Jim Banks was shot in the chest. He couldn't have fired a shot."

"Yes he did, sir. You see, the first rifle bullet missed him altogether. It wangled off something out back in the alley. Mr. Banks drew and fired. Oh, you should have seen him! Even you would have said he was somethin' mighty special with a gun. Anyway, he hit the man with the rifle and then he stepped forward a little and that's when another bullet drilled him straight through the heart."

The boy's eyes betrayed his excitement. "It lifted him off his feet and threw him back against this wall. He was dead before he hit the ground. I didn't even see him twitch."

Clint took a deep breath. He stepped forward and took the kid by the arm and drew him deeper into the shadows. "I want you to go over this whole thing one more time. Start from the beginning and tell it slow.''

''You gonna pay me anything?''

''If I decide that you're telling the truth, yes. But if you lie even a little, I'll know and I'll paddle your ass until it's red. Is that understood?''

''Yes sir! I'd never lie to the Gunsmith. But how much is he going to pay me?''

Clint frowned and dug into his pockets. He was running damn low on money but this was too important a moment to lose, and he did not want to appear stingy. ''Here,'' he said. ''This is a lucky silver medal given to me by the great gunfighter, Herb Dorkman. I killed him in Miles City last year and he said this was given to him by a famous Apache chief named Geronimo.''

Clint saw no need to add that Herb Dorkman, among his other failings, was a notorious liar.

''I heard about Geronimo!'' The boy's eyes widened, and he stared at the silver medal which had something scratched on it that looked like a saguaro cactus only it was growing from both ends. Clint had no idea what kind of Apache sybolism the medal was meant to depict, but its worth based on the price of silver alone was worth more than two dollars.

''Like it?''

''I'll keep it forever,'' the boy whispered. ''Just knowin' it was held by three of the deadliest men in the West gives me the shivers. I feel famous myself just ownin' it.''

''Good! Now go back over your story again, slow.''

Five minutes later, they were back in the alley and Clint was digging a rifle slug out of a rusty stove. The boy was still excited. ''Now are you starting to believe me!''

"Yeah," Clint said, fingering the smashed lead. "Now I believe you. I just wish you'd have seen the second rifleman that shot Mr. Banks dead after the first rifleman botched the job."

"I never even thought that there might have been two. It all happened so fast that I just figured that Mr. Banks was shot by the first one. But I can see now that couldn't have happened. Mr. Banks hit the fella so hard he spun completely around. I was divin' for cover. When I lifted my head up to look around, people were running up to Mr. Banks, just to stare and point at his body and say that, yep, he was sure enough dead."

Clint clapped the boy on the shoulder. "You've been a big help. Now one last thing, point to the place where the first rifleman was hit by Mr. Banks."

"Okay, it was right there between Jewitt's Saddlery and the Onie's Dry Goods Store. The rifleman was standing about two feet back from the boardwalk. I wouldn't even have seen him except for the white puff of rifle smoke when he fired."

"Was he big or small?"

"Bigger'n hell, he was."

"What's your name?"

"Edgar Moffitt."

"Well Edgar, you keep your eyes and ears open. If you think of anything more or hear anything new, let me know."

"You got anymore of these Apache medals?"

"Afraid not."

The boy nodded. "I'll be happy to take money instead."

"Thanks," Clint said as he turned and headed across the street. When he came to the place where the first rifleman was hidden, he knew with dead certainty that Edgar Moffitt had been telling the truth. There was a smear of blood against the dry goods store and dark stains on the ground where blood had seeped into the earth. Clint followed the bloodstains back into the alley and then downhill towards a stable where they disappeared into an old barn.

He drew his gun and entered. "Anyone here!" he called.

"Out back," a voice came to him.

Clint edged through the dim barn and when he came to the rear door, he edged around it carefully to see a fierce-looking old man wearing nothing but bib overalls as he brushed a very handsome black mule. Clint looked the barnyard over carefully, then holstered his gun and stepped outside. "Howdy," he said.

"Howdy."

"You the owner?"

"I am."

"My name is Clint Adams. I'm the new sheriff."

"What happened to lard-ass Hale? He get ventilated?"

"Nope," Clint said. "He got smart and quit."

"You should get smart and quit too. Being a sheriff on the Comstock ain't one bit smart."

"I know," Clint said. "I'm tracking a wounded man. His tracks lead here. Where is he?"

"You must be crazy," the old man said, finally looking up from the mule and glaring at the Gunsmith.

"No I'm not," Clint said. "And if you don't tell me what you know, I'll search every foot of this place until I either find the man or I find evidence enough to arrest you. Which is it going to be?"

In answer, the old man jumped for a pitchfork and he lifted it threateningly. He bent down in a crouch and the hard muscles of his shoulders humped up giving him the appearance of a bulldog ready to attack. "I want no grief, Mister, but unless you pack it on out of here, you're asking for more trouble than you want."

Clint's hand touched the butt of his six-gun. "I can't leave without finding the man who killed Jim Banks early this morning. And in case you aren't smart enough to understand that pitchfork is no match against my six-gun. So are you going to tell me what I want to know or do I search this rat's nest from top to bottom?"

"You must want to die young," the old man growled. "I'm giving you one last chance to get off my property."

Clint just did not understand how this fella could be so stupid! And then it occurred to him that he was not stupid at all. That someone was behind him about to open fire if he didn't walk away.

"All right," Clint said. "I'm leaving. But I'll be back later."

The old man could not hide his surprise. "You're leaving?"

"That's right," Clint said. "I want answers, but not bad enough to kill you and risk getting skewered by that pitchfork."

With that, Clint turned and his eyes looked for a hidden gunman and found him in the hayloft. Clint saw the man's gun poking out from the barn, and he threw himself sideways, drew his own gun and fired.

The man in the loft screamed in pain and his gun tumbled to the earth. Clint heard a roar and turned to see the old man charging him with the pitchfork. The Gunsmith tried to roll, but he was up against the side of the barn. The pitchfork came flying at him and he wanted to duck, but the throw was too low and hard so he just threw his left up to block the fork.

A tine sliced through the heel of his hand and Clint's fingers grabbed the fork and stopped it less than an inch in front of his face. The old man was pulling a knife from his pocket and drawing his arm back to throw when Clint emptied two cylinders of his Colt and stopped him in his tracks. The man's face went slack and he hissed, "Bastard!" Then, he toppled like a weathered oak tree.

Clint knew the stableman was dead and there was no time to waste. Someone was up in the loft and it was the man that had tried to assassinate Jim Banks but had missed and been himself shot.

Clint came to his feet and rushed back into the barn to see the dim outline of a man struggling to climb down from the loft.

"Hold it right there!"

The man froze. He was trapped. A rifle was slung over his broad shoulders, but it was of no use to him while he was hanging onto the ladder.

"Come on down," Clint said. "Slow and easy."

Instead of climbing down one rung at a time, the man fell. It wasn't that much of a fall, maybe only about eight feet, but he hit hard and didn't move. Clint knew that he was badly wounded.

"Frankie," he said as he rolled the big man over and stared at his ashen face. "I should have guessed it was either you or one of the other two that Rick keeps on his leash. Why did you try to kill Jim Banks this morning?"

"Water," the man wheezed. "I need water."

Clint twisted around and saw a water barrel across the barn. He turned and looked back down at Frankie. There was a hole in the bouncer's gut and Clint did not have to be told that the man was going to die and that he was in agony. "Who hired you to kill Jim Banks and then shot you when you missed?"

"First . . . the water," Frankie said between clenched teeth.

Clint went for the water. But when he reached the barrel, he discovered that it was empty. He hurried outside and found a horse trough, then removed his Stetson and filled it with water. Rushing back into the dim interior of the barn, he suddenly had a sense that something was terribly amiss.

Frankie had managed to sit up and grip his rifle. He pulled it up to his shoulder, took unsteady aim and fired just as Clint hurled his Stetson at the man and dove into a pile of loose straw.

Frankie's bullet ripped a hole through the Stetson and sent water cascading into the air. The man cursed, tried to lever another shell into the chamber and that's when Clint reversed directions, poked his gun out of the straw pile and yelled, "Drop it or you're dead!"

"I'm already dead, you son of a bitch!" Frankie screamed as he took aim.

With great reluctance, Clint shot the man. He aimed for the shoulder but there was no time for refinements so that, when he saw Frankie take the bullet and slump over, Clint knew that he had cut it a little too fine.

He crawled out of the pile of straw and rushed to Frankie's side. Grabbing him by the hair, he raised his head and stared into sightless eyes.

"Aw dammit!" the Gunsmith wailed, as he dropped the head and stood up to reload his gun. "Dammit anyway!"

The Gunsmith was fit to be tied. He'd had two men who could have put the finger on Rick Hadley and now they were both dead. So here he was again back at square one with no place to turn. He hadn't gained a damn thing for all this risk and his trouble except for a wounded hand that suddenly began to throb.

"Drop your gun, Clint!"

Clint turned on his heel and saw Rick Hadley and his two remaining bouncers standing at the entrance to the barn. All three were holding double-barreled shotguns, and there wasn't a chance in the world that they'd miss if they pulled their triggers. Clint did the only thing he could do under the circumstances, he dropped his gun.

"You're under arrest for the murder of these two men," Rick said as a crowd began to gather behind him. "You killed Mr. Puckett and his son Frankie. I reckon the evidence just dropped beside your feet. Turn around slow and easy."

"Quite a coincidence you and your two friends just happened to be here with shotguns, isn't it?"

"Some people learn to be in the right place at the right time and some don't," Rick said. "You were warned to leave the Comstock. Instead, you went on a bloody killing spree and now I have a hunch that you'll never leave the Comstock—you'll be buried in it."

Clint shook his head. "I guess you've outsmarted me this time," he said. "And as always, your luck is still holding."

"And yours isn't," Rick said. "Tough break. Now turn around or I'll kill you where you stand."

Clint knew Rick and knew that he wasn't bluffing. He turned around and a moment later, a rope was looped around his chest pinning his arms to his sides. He was bound up and shoved back out into the sunlight. There were at least a hundred men filling the barnyard and some of them were ready for a necktie party.

"They'll be no lynching!" Rick shouted. "It's time we had some law in this town. Sheriff Hale has quit and I am nominating my friend and employee, Max Bullock, for the job. Does anyone have any objections?"

The crowd roared that it did not. Max Bullock, one of the two remaining bouncers, shoved Clint to the ground, then yanked him back to his feet and hissed, "Frankie was my best friend. You're gonna pay bad before we string you up and let you swing in the wind."

Clint said nothing. He was shoved and punched and goaded up the street to the jail and then tossed inside and locked up. Outside, men were shouting and waving hangman's ropes.

Clint looked through the bars. "Why don't you let them take me, Rick?"

Rick turned and he was smiling. "I just might. But first, the new sheriff of Gold Hill, Nevada has to at least make a show of protecting you, doesn't he?"

Clint nodded and lay down on the thin straw mattress that served as his bunk. "Yeah," he said quietly, "I guess he does at that."

FOURTEEN

Miss Miranda Hale heard the news about Clint's arrest almost as soon as the Gunsmith was thrown in the Gold Hill jail because it swept through the Comstock like a prairie fire. Most of the miners had not even realized that the famed Gunsmith was on the Comstock, and when it was learned he had killed old man Puckett and his son Frankie, there was a mixed but spirited reaction. Most thought the Gunsmith deserved a medal because Puckett had been an irracible old man with a mean streak that he'd passed on to his son Frankie. Many who had lived on the Comstock over the years well remembered both father and son clearing out entire saloons. Frankie had killed two men with his bare hands, and his father had bragged of killing a lot more. Because of their reputations, it was generally agreed that everyone gained by having the damned Pucketts buried. Still, murder was murder, and if the Gunsmith were to hang in Virginia City, it would be the greatest spectacle since a topless, three-hundred-pound fat lady had ridden a two-humped camel from Silver City to Reno in order to promote her questionable services.

Miranda had managed to forget about the fat lady, but she knew that she could not live with her own conscience if she did not visit the man who had treated her with respect and kindness. And deep down, she did not believe he would have simply gunned the awful Pucketts down without good cause.

"I have to go," she told her father.

"I should go with you," he said, looking up from one of the dime novels he was constantly reading.

"Then put on your boots and let's go," Miranda said. "He did you a favor when he took your office. He promised to help you find some other work if he could, and you called him a legend. I think that he deserves a little support."

Hale stood up and swallowed. "Well," he hedged. "I'd go but I'm just not sure it would be in the Gunsmith's best interests. You see, me being the former sheriff and all, it might make things tougher on him in the long run."

Miranda's eyes sparked with anger. "How could it get any tougher! You know that Rick and everyone else who has a grudge against Clint will hire some bogus judge to come up here and preside over a kangaroo court. They'll hang him for sure!"

Hale agreed but said, "Still, it seems pretty certain that he did shoot the Pucketts."

"They deserved to be shot!" Miranda retorted angrily. "Remember the time that Frankie grabbed and manhandled me at the dance? You had to pull a gun on him, and even then he didn't want to let go. He challenged you to step outside."

"I wish now I'd have shot him," Hale said, trying to dredge up some anger. "I should have killed him for touching you."

Miranda's voice softened. "No, you shouldn't have. But he should have been arrested and thrown in jail for awhile."

"I didn't want to make Rick mad. I thought I needed that job. Maybe I still do."

"No," she said quickly. "You'll find something

better. We have some savings in the bank. I am starting work next week at the millinery shop on D street. We'll get by.''

"What about Rick? If he learns you visited the Gunsmith, he'll be sore as could be. He might even break off the engagement. Then where'd you be?''

"I'd be worlds better off,'' Miranda said. "I'm not waiting for Rick to break off our engagement. I'm going to do it myself.''

"Now . . .''

"I've made up my mind,'' Miranda said in a firm voice that left no doubt she could not be swayed from her decision.

Her father shook his head. "You're throwin' away the chance to have money. You'll never have a better chance than this, and you're throwing it all away for nothin'.''

"Nothing but peace of mind. I've decided I'd rather be poor than marry a man who strikes women and cheats on them at the same time. It's no life, father. I'd never be able to trust him for a minute. I'd probably wind up throwing myself out a window, if he didn't leave me first.''

The ex-sheriff nodded. "I suppose you're right. Anyway, I do have to admire your courage. Your mother had courage.''

"And so did you,'' she said, feeling suddenly much stronger than her father and wanting to comfort him. "Mother said you were the bravest man she ever knew.''

His eyes glistened and he looked down at one of his worn dime novels resting on the arm of their threadbare couch. "I got old before my time being a sheriff, Miranda. Old and tired and scared. It just happened before I even realized it. I . . .''

Miranda touched her father's lips. "Sit down and

read your book," she told him. "I'll give your regards to Clint when I see him. I'll tell him we plan to help him in any way that we can."

Hale nodded. He looked ashamed and, at the same time, immensely relieved that he would not have to go back to the sheriff's office. He just wanted to be left alone.

Miranda hurried down to the business district of Gold Hill. She did not want to think about her father anymore today. His eyes were haunted and fearful. She had assumed that once he was out of office he would immediately relax and even regain a little of his former cheerfulness. That had not happened so far. He was still afraid of Rick Hadley, especially now that she had decided to break their engagement. But why?

The only reason that Miranda could think of was that her father knew something very bad about Rick. Something serious enough to send even him to prison. As long as he was a prospective father-in-law, he must have figured he was safe. But now . . . now he was just a frightened ex-sheriff who knew too much.

Miranda expelled a deep breath. She had the beginning of an idea. She would somehow help Clint Adams escape from the gallows and, in return, he would help her and her father escape the Comstock. After all, Clint was famous. He had been written about in many novels. He would have rich friends and connections and, surely, one of them would give her father some kind of honest work.

"Clint needs us and we need him," she reminded herself out loud as she approached the jail. "It is just a matter of mutual necessities."

Miranda stopped across the street from the jail and studied the angry mob that was swilling free beer supplied by Rick's saloon and working itself up to

lynch Clint, probably as soon as the sun went down.
Jackals, Miranda had heard, always waited to do
their bloody work in the darkness.

She was more frightened than she cared to admit.
Not only would she have to endure the heckling of
an increasingly drunken and dangerous crowd of
miners, but she would also have to face whoever
was inside guarding Clint Adams. Miranda brushed
an errant tendril of hair from her eyes and steeled her
nerves.

"Your hair looks fine as always," Honey said
coming up behind her. "Why don't you go to the
church social they're having today up in Virginia
City and leave Clint and me to work things out?"

Miranda's first impulse was to tell this woman
that she could go jump in the horse trough and soak
her head, but good sense stopped her. "I know you
don't like me and I'm not overly fond of you either,
Miss Day, but it seems we both like Clint Adams
and he is in a bad fix. Maybe we ought to discuss
the options we have to getting him out before that
mob drags him out and hangs him."

Honey studied the crowd. "Even if I undressed in
the street and sang a song and danced so my tits
flopped around, it wouldn't divert their intentions
long enough for you or anyone else to get Clint out
of that jail."

Miranda was shocked by such descriptive language. Yet, it occurred to her that such language had
to be expected from this saloon singer and woman of
low morals. Also, it was probably the God's honest
truth. The mob was definitely in a killing mood.

"All right," she said. "We rule out a diversion.
That leaves us almost no options."

"We have to get into that jail and then try and get
the drop on that ox, Max Bullock. He's not very

bright. I'm sure we could do it and then open the cell door.''

"But that wouldn't help us at all," Miranda said. "I've spent a lot of time in that jail with my father. Not only isn't there a back door, there's not a weak place in the walls or a window other than the two we can see from the front, and they wouldn't help us get Clint out.''

"Why are you helping him in the first place?" Honey demanded. "You got Rick. He'll make you rich if he doesn't get himself killed.''

"Clint is no murderer," Miranda said. "I'm not arguing that he shot the Pucketts, but I know he did it in self-defense.''

"Of course he did," Honey said. "But if Rick finds out you betrayed him, there's no telling what he'll do to you.''

Miranda lifted her chin. "You face the same risk. You're his woman. You know him even better than I do.''

"He'd have us both shot," Honey said. "Rick won't stand for being turned on. I've seen what he can do.''

Miranda did not want to hear anymore about it. "We can talk about Rick some other time," she said. "Right now, we have to get Clint out of that cell before his time has run out.''

"It'll take a miracle," Honey said.

Miranda thought about that for a minute and then she smiled.

"No, I think it will take deception.''

"What is that supposed to mean?''

"I've got an idea," she said, pulling the woman close. "But only *you* can tell me if it's worth a try.''

FIFTEEN

Joel P. Boswell was a Shakespearean actor, or so he claimed. He was tall, wore a frock coat and stovepipe hat, but it was plain to see that he was gaunt to the point of emaciation, and he had obviously fallen on hard times. Once, he had shown great promise on the stage, but that was twenty years ago and now his voice was a little too hoarse, the result of too much whiskey and too many cheap cigars. His cuffs were frayed and his gold pocket watch had long since been hocked for one of cheaper material. Nowadays, he stood in saloons and on street corners and recited Shakespeare to passersby. His once proud stovepipe had become the repository for whatever coins the more generous and appreciative of his audience might toss. At other times he would help around Piper's Opera House. He would coach the newcomers, do their makeup and hair, or even sweep out the place if that was required to earn himself a ticket and a few dollars.

Sitting on the porch of the great Piper's Opera House, Joel again recounted his downfall to Miranda and Honey, the two most beautiful women on the Comstock Lode.

"It was women and whiskey," he lamented. "I should have been famous! I had one of the greatest voices in the world, and my sense of timing, my sheer theatrical presence was like a magnet. Women swooned over me in my glorious prime, rich patrons begged to be my friend. I had the world at my feet.''

Honey sighed. ''I know what you mean. Two weeks ago, Rick Hadley swore I would become the queen of the Comstock. Now, he says I haven't the talent.''

''You don't,'' Joel said without malice. ''I'm sorry, but you do not. You have the body and the ambition, but not the voice. Me, I had it all.''

Miranda bridled her growing impatience. ''We have a proposition for you, Mr. Boswell.''

''I am too old to proposition,'' he said. ''Even by a pair as beautiful as you.''

''It's not that kind of a proposition,'' Honey said. ''We want to hire your services.''

He brightened. ''You mean you want me to do a one-man Shakespearian play? I can, you know. Which would you like? Name one! *King Lear, Hamlet,* or perhaps—''

''I'm afraid that we need your makeup skills and we need them right now,'' Miranda said, growing nervous with the quick passage of time. It was nearly sundown and the mob would be getting bolder by the minute. ''We need you to make up Clint Adams so that we can spring him from jail.''

Boswell blinked. ''Preposterous!''

''No,'' Honey said. ''It would be an act of justice. A great triumph and a monument to your makeup skills if you could pull it off. We need him to look like me.''

Boswell studied both their faces, certain that they were teasing him. ''You must be insane.''

''We are desperate,'' Honey said. ''The Gunsmith is famous. If you do this, you would be famous too because we will tell it to the press when he is exonerated of all wrongdoing. It will be written up all over the country and your name will become a legend just for saving a legend.''

"That's right," Miranda added. "You will become the stuff of my father's dime novels."

"Are you serious?" Boswell swallowed. "Yes, I can see you are serious. I would become a celebrity! Perhaps, if I had a little acclaim, I might even stage a comeback.''

"Anything is possible," Honey said. "But time is running out. There is a mob working itself up to a lynching party. We have to go through it, get inside, overpower Max and . . .''

"Oh, no we don't!" Boswell said, throwing his hands up in protest. "It would be a worthy goal to free Clint Adams and earn back my self-respect, but not worthy enough to risk my life against a lout such as Max. He would tear my head off!''

"I've got a derringer," Honey said. "It will be easy to get the drop on him and then, once the door is open, Clint can dispose of him.''

"You mean, murder him?''

"Of course not," Miranda said. "Just tap him on the head and put him to sleep for awhile.''

"Oh," Boswell said. "And then what happens? He'll remember I was with you and figure out what happened. I'll be shot or else sent to prison as an accomplice.''

Boswell folded up his thin arms and said, "No. No. No.''

Honey looked at Miranda who looked down at the broach she was wearing. "This is an heirloom," she said. "It is made out of solid silver and belonged to my dear grandmother. It is worth at least a hundred dollars.''

"Hmmm," Boswell said, reaching out to touch it.

"The woman obviously had excellent taste. Was she beautiful like you?"

"Much prettier," Miranda said. "Will you take it in lieu of money?"

"I cannot, my dear."

"But why?"

"It is simply that a broach will not save me from being shot or hung by a lynch mob."

"Oh for cripe's sakes!" Honey swore. She reached into her purse and began to extract money as Boswell licked his lips.

"There," Honey said. "A hundred and one dollars and two bits. That's enough to get you out of Virginia City and back to New York where there are dozens of playhouses."

Boswell snatched up the money and then he extended his palm up for the broach. "With money, I can now accept your dear grandmother's gift."

Miranda handed it back to him.

Noting her reluctance, Boswell said, "I am sorry I can't refuse to take this. You see, my dear, I have fallen on hard times as you may have surmised. But you have youth and beauty, both far more valuable commodities than any other you will ever receive. A beautiful woman can always find a way to recoup her loses, but an old Shakespearian actor . . . well, it's not so easy."

Miranda understood. "Then we have a deal?"

"Yes. I will meet you at the sheriff's office and we—"

"Oh, no!" Honey grabbed him by the sleeve and pulled out her derringer. "You'll stay with us until this is over."

Boswell forced a weak grin. "Of course, my dear!"

"Then git moving. We'll be right behind you."

Boswell led them down the street until he came to

a small shack. "This, I'm ashamed to say, is my humble abode. Will you wait outside while I get my kit of makeup, wigs and other tricks?"

"All right," Miranda said, "but please hurry!"

Boswell disappeared through a door that hung on one rusty hinge. He closed the door carefully behind him and then Honey tiptoed around the shack to catch the man sneaking out the back through a broken board. "Get back in there, and if you aren't out in two minutes, we'll come in and drag you out!" she said angrily.

Boswell, whose head and shoulders had been sticking out through the wall, disappeared with a shriek of humiliation.

Ten minutes later, they were striding through the well-lubricated crowd and entering the sheriff's office amidst hoots and whistles.

Max Bullock was sitting behind the sheriff's desk looking very pleased with himself until they barged inside. "What do you want!" he demanded. "You can't . . ."

Honey pulled out the derringer. "One word. One shout of warning and you're dead."

"You wouldn't dare!" Max said roughly. "The crowd would rush in here just as soon as they heard the shot."

"I'd say that you went crazy and shot yourself," Honey told him.

"That's the dumbest thing I ever heard of," Boswell stammered.

"Unless you can come up with something much better," Miranda hissed, "please shut up."

"That's telling him!" Honey said, her voice filled with new found admiration. "If you stick with me awhile, you'll come up with more spunk than you ever thought possible."

"I've always had plenty of spunk," Miranda snapped, as she marched over to the rifle case and grabbed a double-barreled shotgun. "Sheriff, she'll shoot you dead if you don't help us, and if you aren't finished quick, I'll blow your brains out with this, so help me God!"

The sight of the big shotgun was far more intimidating than that of the derringer and Max moved quickly. "All right, all right! You women take it easy and I'll get the keys. But when Rick finds out what you did, you're both finished anyway. And Boswell, I'm going to—"

"Move it!" Miranda said, pushing the shotgun at him hard.

The sheriff moved quickly to the cell, and Clint was grinning from ear to ear when the lock turned and he was set free. "You ladies sure came in the nick of time," he said, striding past the sheriff to peer through the closed curtains at the milling crowd outside. "But I'm not sure that what you did was very smart. A tribe of Apaches couldn't break through that murdering crowd."

"We have a plan," Miranda said. "Sit down at the desk and let Mr. Boswell transform you into a woman."

Clint's eyebrows raised in question until Boswell reached inside of his bag and produced a wig, a dress and a large selection of rouges, lipsticks, eye-liners and other cosmetic aides.

"I don't believe this," Clint groaned.

"There's no other way," Miranda told him. "There is only one exit and that is through that crowd outside."

Clint looked into Boswell's bloodshot eyes. "Are you good enough to pull this off?"

The man raised his chin. "Yes," he said. "Now sit down."

Clint grinned, then he found his six-gun in the sheriff's drawer. He made certain that it was still loaded, then he turned and smashed Max across the side of the head. The big man's eyes rolled up, and he crumpled like a wet paper sack. Clint caught him and dragged him into the cell and locked it. "Hide the key," he said, pitching it to Miranda before he took his seat behind the sheriff's desk.

Boswell was good and he was fast. He had done hundreds of cosmetic changes between acts, and the first thing he did was to powder the Gunsmith's face and then apply eye makeup. Lipstick followed, and after a few deft touches with his cosmetics, he slapped on the wig and carefully arranged it on Clint's head.

"You aren't going to pose any competition for Miss Honey and Miss Miranda," he said, grabbing the dress from his bag and stuffing newspapers into the front. "And you aren't even going to be a raving beauty. But with bad light and those men outside half drunk, I think this will work."

"It has to work," Clint said. "But what about the rest of you?"

"I'm staying," Honey said. "Me too," Miranda added.

Clint frowned. "Not a chance," he said. "We are all going out together and we are going out fast. We'll leave the door open and, if everything goes as I have seen in the past, this crowd will rush the door and pile in on itself so that those in front can't get out and stop our escape. There will be confusion and shouting."

"With Max the only one left in here, maybe they'll decide to lynch him for the sheer sport of it," Honey said.

"Turn your backs for a minute," Clint ordered, as he unbuckled his pants.

"Must we?" Honey asked. "This ought to be real cute."

Clint was in no mood for levity. "Now!"

They turned their backs and the Gunsmith undressed quickly. It felt ridiculous climbing into a dress but he had no choice and since his life was at stake, he did not complain.

"All right," he said. "Let's go. Don't anyone stop and don't bother to answer questions. Just keep moving."

"I'm coming with you," Boswell said. "And I'm staying with you until we get safely off the Comstock Lode. I'm a dead man here."

No one said anything to that because it was probably the truth. "Miranda, you and Honey go first and then you go next, Mr. Boswell. I'll leave the door open and come last."

"Are you sure?"

"Yes," Clint said, shoving his six-gun into the dress pocket. "If anyone tries to stop me, I'll shoot to wound. But if that happens, run for your lives."

The three of them nodded. Clint looked back at the unconscious sheriff. "All right," he said tersely, "let's go!"

Honey threw the door open and hurried out. The crowd surged forward and someone drunkenly made a grab for her, but Honey was still carrying her derringer in her fist and smacked him alongside the head and he wobbled. "Out of my way!" she cried, as the mob parted for her and the rest of them.

Clint left the door open and someone yelled, "Let's get in there and lynch him!"

The crowd pushed forward as men streamed up and out of the street to pour into the sheriff's office.

Clint heard the first shouts of confusion and anger as the mob discovered he was missing and, in his place, there was just the unconscious Max Bullock.

"Let's make a run for it!" he shouted.

Old Boswell and the two women did not have to be told twice. They ran into the darkness, and wearing a dress, Clint Adams was damned hard pressed just to keep up.

SIXTEEN

Clint waited only until he rounded the corner before he stopped and tore the buttons off his dress, then, hopping around on one leg, finally kicked his way out of the thing and continued after Miranda, Honey and old Boswell who was surprisingly fleet for his age and condition.

"Where are we going!" Clint panted. "There's no time to saddle horses. That mob would be on us before we could get out of town."

Honey stopped, bent over and gasped for air. She was more voluptuous than Miranda and not nearly in as good a running condition. "I can't . . . can't go a step farther," she wheezed.

Clint took one of her arms and said, "Yes you can. And I won't leave you until we are off the Comstock. You're in this up to your lovely neck, Honey. When Rick finds out you and his fiancée both betrayed him to save me, there will be pure hell to pay."

"I'll take my chances," she cried.

"No you won't," Clint said. "And as for getting off the Comstock alive, I think our only chance is to run east toward the V. & T. train station just below Virginia City."

"But even as the crow flies, that's still better than a mile!" Honey protested.

"You can make it," Clint said, pulling the woman through the sagebrush. "It's just over the hill and down the other side a little ways. They'll have all the roads blocked within a few minutes, but we might just make it out on the train."

As soon as they were over the hill and out of sight, Clint pulled up and let Honey catch her breath. "What time is it?" he asked.

Boswell pulled his watch out of his vest pocket and peered closely at it in the moonlight. "Nine o'clock."

Miranda said, "A train does leave about ten."

"It's our only hope," Clint said.

But Boswell disagreed. "I think they'll check the depot before they allow the train to depart. I know I would if I were looking for the four of us."

"We'll just have to trust that we can get on it safely," Clint said, "unless anyone has any better ideas."

Clint could see the lights of Virginia City spread out before him. "Who is Fr. Doolin?"

"He's the pastor of St. Mary's of the Mountains. That huge Catholic church that stands along the railroad tracks. Look, you can see the tall steeple in the moonlight from here."

"Do you really think he will help?"

"I don't know," Miranda said. "I'm not Catholic, but I've met him any number of times, and we have worked on some charities together."

Boswell nodded. "He's fed me a time or two when things got to be their worst. He's a good man. Not too pious to share with a man a drop of the dew of old Ireland."

"All right then," Clint said. "It appears that we have little choice. I doubt we have more than a few minutes left before they start coming. Let's just hope that Fr. Doolin is a brave and charitable man, one willing to help those not of his faith.''

''Or any other faith,'' Honey said. ''I never believed in God.''

''Well you don't have to tell the good padre that,'' Clint said, pulling Honey along as they rushed down the rock and brush mountainside toward the huge brick church with its great spiked steeple. When they reached the church, they found that it was unlocked.

Clint entered first, completely forgetting how ridiculous he must have looked without his pants so that his long underwear was showing. The others followed. The interior of the church was pure Gothic, with a hand carved main altar, a beautiful seventeenth-century Florentine painting and high ceiling beams supported by massive columns. There were at least forty rows of pews and, up in the front, perhaps a dozen of the most faithful were on their knees praying.

Clint placed his finger to his lips to indicate that they were to be very quiet. He took a deep breath, unsure of what he was supposed to do. Ducking his head back out the front door, he caught a glimpse of an angry mob coming down the hill.

''The confessional boxes!'' Boswell cried. ''They are our only hope.''

Clint knew the man was right. ''Where are they?''

Boswell pointed and whispered, ''I was raised Episcopalian but there isn't much difference. No one will search the confessionals if they feel that they're in use.''

Clint and the women followed Boswell up the side aisles. The floors of the church were of polished hardwood, but they squeaked mightily.

''Here,'' Boswell said, ''there are two of them. We'll have to double up.''

Clint was skeptical, and when he opened the door, an old woman was on her knees in prayer. She looked at Clint standing in his long underwear and cried, "Dear Lord, how did you know this is what I been sinful thinkin' about!"

Miranda's cheeks reddened and she said, "Miss Kawalski, please excuse us but this poor sinner is in a terrible hurry to make his confession. Could we please ask you to step out right now?"

The old woman was dumbstruck. She nodded and bolted into the aisle, slammed into a pew and raced toward the front door. Clint's attention was captured for a moment by Boswell who was shoving Honey into the other confessional. The old Shakespearean had a wicked gleam in his eye, and Clint figured that Honey would have her hands full with the man.

"Come on!" Miranda said with some urgency. "They could come rushing through the front door any minute!"

Clint jammed into the confessional box with Miranda and closed the door tight. It was pitch black and they stood pressed close together, both listening for the sounds of a mob coming into the church. But all they heard was their own breathing, the soft chanting of the faithful who prayed the rosary and an occasional cough.

As the minutes passed, Clint grew increasingly uncomfortable trying to keep back from Miranda. "I hope we don't have to spend too much time locked up in here," he said.

In reply, Miranda laid her head against his chest and whispered, "It could be a lot worse. We could be hanging from underneath a railroad car or hiding in some spooky old mine shaft. I can think of a lot more unpleasant things than this."

"So can I," Clint admitted, slipping his arms around the sheriff's daughter and explaining, "this is a lot more comfortable."

Miranda turned her face up to him and her mouth

found his and they kissed with a passion entirely inappropriate for their spiritual surroundings. Miranda snuggled close and said, "No one would believe this if we told them."

"I know," Clint said. "And can you imagine what is going on in the confessional next to us? I'll bet old Boswell is trying to find his lost youth."

Miranda giggled. "I'm sure you're right. Honey could rejuvenate anyone. But then, I'm not telling you anything that you didn't already know, am I?"

Clint supposed that it would be pressing his luck if he lied in a confessional where so many purer hearts had unburdened themselves of their sins. "No," he said, "I've had the pleasure of Miss Honey."

"I'm very grateful you didn't try to lie to me about that," Miranda said. "Rick has lied about her for years, it's nice to hear honesty for a change. Clint?"

"What?"

"If we get off the Comstock, will you help my father?"

"How?"

"I don't know," she admitted. "I fear for his life. I'm afraid that he is privy to something dishonest that Rick has done. Something important enough that his life might be in danger. I'd just feel better if he lived far away, and I thought you might know some people with money who might need some security for their ranch or business. He wouldn't require much in the way of a salary. He doesn't drink and he's conscientious."

"I think I can find him something he'd enjoy," the Gunsmith said. "But what about you?"

"I'll get along."

"You could ride with me awhile."

Miranda kissed him again, and the heat from her body fired Clint. His hand came up and he began to unbutton her blouse when suddenly, a voice came through a little screen and said, "Child of God, are you ready for the sacred act of contrition?"

Clint jerked his hand away so violently that his elbow crashed into the side of the box.

There was a moment of silence and the priest said, "Please be calm. This is between us and God. No matter what you have done, my son, it will be forgiven if you truly repent of your sins."

Clint cleared his throat. His mind was racing and, in the end, Miranda saved him. "Father Doolin," she began, "I'm afraid that we are not here to give a confession."

"We?" he asked, his voice filled with astonishment. "Are you saying that there are more than one of you in the box right now?"

"Yes," Miranda said. "Furthermore, we are not even Catholic."

"My God!" the priest exclaimed. "Then what are you doing . . . no, never mind. I can guess. God help you for this blasphemous sin committed in His house!"

"Father," Clint interceded, "we just kissed a couple of times, honest. And we *are* in trouble."

"That is for sure!"

"No," Clint said, "not just with the Lord, but with the town. You see, I am the Gunsmith, and the woman in my arms helped me escape from jail."

"I don't want to hear this," Fr. Doolin groaned. "It has already been a very long and difficult day."

"Father, please," Miranda pleaded. "This is a real emergency. I'm Miranda Hale. My father was the sheriff of Gold Hill and I know we've met before."

"Yes," the priest said. "I remember you now."

"Our lives are in great danger," Miranda said. "A lynch mob was about to hang the Gunsmith, and I had to free him. And if you don't help us, then we are all lost."

The priest sighed. "What do you want?"

"Sanctuary," Clint said, "sanctuary until the V. & T. Railroad train pulls out at ten o'clock."

"You killed two men. I heard about it in town."

"In self-defense," Clint said. "Now, I realize that I broke one of the Ten Commandments, but I had no choice. And I am to be hung if you won't help us. Father, the mob might even hang Miss Hale for helping spring me from jail."

"Then I have no choice," the priest said after several long minutes of prayer and reflection. "Of course I will help you."

"Thank you, Father," both Clint and Miranda said at the same time.

"You are welcome," the priest said. "Now, as long as you are here, and even though you are not Catholic, I think it only right and pleasing to God that you make confessions."

"What!" Clint could not believe his ears. "Father, that's not fair."

"It sure isn't," Miranda said with exasperation in her voice.

"Fair has nothing to do with it," the priest said patiently. "You came for sanctuary to the Lord's house and you must understand that the only thing He asks in repayment is simple, heartfelt confessions. Now, which one of you is going to go first."

"You go," Miranda said quickly.

Clint did not want to make a confession but he was trapped. "Father, I have sinned all my life. Not bad sins. Oh, I've killed a lot of men, but—"

"And those are not bad sins?"

"I only killed those that needed killing," Clint insisted, even though the words sounded hollow in his own ears. "And I never cheated anyone. Not ever. I am a good friend and—"

"Please," the priest said, "this is a confessional,

not a testimonial to your questionable virtues, Mr. Gunsmith! Let us make our act of contrition with humble and repentant hearts. Begin please.''

Clint felt Miranda begin to shake with the giggles. ''What's so damned funny?'' he demanded.

''Nothing,'' she said. ''Except that I have a feeling your sins will take more than two hours, and I'll get off free.''

''Don't count on it,'' Clint said in a huff. ''I'll keep it to the bare essentials and I'll talk fast.''

''The Lord will accept that,'' Fr. Doolin said. ''Now please begin at the beginning.''

Clint searched back over the years to his boyhood. ''Well, the first mean thing I ever remember was shoving a stick of dynamite into old Charley Hannah's outhouse while he was reading inside, and then watching the shit and Charley come flying out all at the same time.''

''Oh God,'' the priest groaned. ''You are going to be *bad*.''

Clint grinned in the darkness. He could see that baring of his soul might have its bright moments after all. ''Well Father, you and the Lord asked for it straight, so here goes.''

He had just gotten started when he heard a loud crash outside. Clint's words froze on his lips and the priest whispered, ''I think I had better attend to our visitors.''

The door squeaked open and then shut, and the priest's footsteps could be heard moving down the wooden floor. Clint pushed the door to their confessional open just a crack and peered out.

''What is going on?'' Miranda whispered.

''It's them, all right. They're angry and demanding to search the church from top to bottom. The priest is refusing them.''

"Good!" Miranda said. "Good for him."

"Uh-oh, the mob has shoved past the priest. They're going to do their search anyway. We're as good as hung," Clint said, dragging his gun out of his long underwear.

But Fr. Doolin surprised him. The priest hurried along in front of the advancing mob, his voice was angry. "You may search behind the sacristy, but you cannot desecrate this church or its worshipers with your barbarism. I and Fr. O'Grady are hearing confessions and you must not disturb us again!"

Clint closed the door. He heard the searchers stomp past the confessionals, and then he heard the door close as Fr. Doolin climbed back inside. "I have also broken the commandment about lying," he said in a sad voice. "I must pray for forgiveness."

"The Lord will forgive you," Clint said. "And if you measure good deeds in the number of lives saved, then you are really a savior because I'd not have let them take us without a bad fight."

The priest sighed. "I mean no offense, Mr. Gunsmith, but I see no point in hearing any more of your shocking confession, or even starting yours, Miss Hale. I think you both are beyond immediate hope. Perhaps, if we had more time . . ."

"That's all right," Clint interrupted. "As soon as the mob leaves, we can all go."

"What do you mean, 'all' go?"

"There are two more in the other confessional."

Fr. Doolin made a small, strange sound of despair, and then he began to pray his own rosary.

SEVENTEEN

The shrill sound of the Virginia & Truckee's steam whistle cut through the thin, high desert air.

Miranda said, "The train is ready to leave. It ought to be passing by here in two or three minutes."

Clint nodded. "Padre, I appreciate all that you did for us. If you want to offer a prayer for our escape from the Comstock, that will be fine with me."

"And if you somehow manage to escape, what then?" he asked, looking at each one of them.

"I'm on my way to New York City," Boswell said. "I plan to sell the story of all this to a Broadway agent. Someone will write a dime novel on it and I'll star in a Wild West play. It could be my ticket to fame."

"And you, Miss Day?"

Honey looked at Clint and then at Miranda. "I think my plans have just changed. Maybe I'll go to New York, too. I ought to be able to find honest work on Broadway, if this old Shakespearian devil will give me a few acting lessons."

"I surely will!" Boswell said, his face a little flushed and excited.

"I mean *real* acting lessons," she said. "What you were doing in there was no act, you lecher!"

The priest shook his head. "I don't want to hear another word about it," he said. "Miranda, what about you and your father?"

Miranda looked at the Gunsmith. "Clint has promised to help both of us," she said. "My father's life may be in jeopardy. He needs to get off the Comstock."

"That's my job," Clint said. "Once things cool down a little, I'm coming back for Sheriff Hale, Rick Hadley's scalp and my horse and gear."

"Perhaps that would be very unwise," the priest said. "I see no need for bloodshed, and Rick Hadley has been generous to many charitable causes. I cannot believe that he is evil or dangerous."

Clint knew that anything he said would not be believed. It was very likely that Rick had even contributed to some charity promoted by the good padre. "So long," Clint said, "and thanks for the pants. I was feeling pretty ridiculous walking around in my underwear."

He moved outside. Fortunately, a thin gauzy layer of clouds partly obscured a full moon. He could see the train's huge silhouette and its puffing clouds of steam that rose toward the stars. Clint also saw a few men still prowling along the slopes both above and below the tracks searching for him and his friends.

"It won't be easy," he said. "In fact, I'm afraid that, without a diversion, it won't even be possible."

Miranda turned to the priest. "If you could ring the steeple bell at just the right moment, then we could escape and there would be no shooting."

"You want me to wake up the children of the town?"

Clint frowned. "Better they wake up to the sound of your bell than to the sound of my gunfire."

"True," the priest admitted. "All right, I'll do it."

Clint grinned. "Thanks again."

He led the others around to the side of the church

and then, when he thought the coast was clear, he led them in a dash for a small tool shed down by the tracks.

Honey was the slowest, and she was almost spotted before Clint ran back and dragged her the last fifty yards. Panting and fighting for breath, she said, "I'm just not made for this running stuff!"

"You're doing fine," Clint said, his eyes tracking the searchers as well as the train which was beginning to come toward them.

The tool shed was only about forty feet from the tracks, but there were two searchers who were sharing a bottle of whiskey and blocking the way. "If they don't move, I'll have to take them out however I can," Clint said tightly. "I hope the padre remembers his promise to ring his steeple bell."

"He will," Miranda said.

And just then, the steeple bell began to clang so loudly that it even drowned out the sound of the steam engine.

The two drinking men stood up, both swaying. One yelled, "What the hell is a church bell ringing for at this hour of the night!"

"Hell if I know! Maybe it means there's a fire or somethin'. We better go find out!"

"Hell, we drank so much whiskey and ale tonight we can piss away any old church fire!"

Clint grinned as the pair staggered off toward the church. "I can see now that those two wouldn't have been too much of a problem. Let's go!"

He grabbed both Honey and Miranda by the hand, and they dashed for the tracks with Boswell pulling out well ahead of them. The train was picking up speed faster than Clint had expected because it was going downhill and they really had to push to reach the tracks.

Boswell vaulted onto the side of a boxcar and hung suspended out over the track for an instant before he pulled himself inside.

"We'll only have one chance at this!" Clint shouted, trying to make his voice heard over the thundering of the train. "We can't afford to miss."

"I can't do it!" Honey cried. "I'll fall under the wheels and be cut in two!"

"No you won't!"

"Yes I will," she sobbed, running along beside the railroad cars which were already starting to pass them faster and faster.

"Jump!" Clint shouted to the two women as a flatcar came rushing at them from out of the darkness.

Miranda had no trouble at all, but it was clear to the Gunsmith that poor Honey just did not have the strength left in her flagging body to throw herself over the lip of the flatcar.

So he grabbed her and, with a wrenching motion of his body, he hurled the frightened woman upward. He heard her screaming as she vanished for an instant against the blurring background of the train, and then her white petticoats told him that she had made it safely up on top and not rolled over the other side.

The only problem was that, in throwing the woman on the run, Clint had lost his own balance and fallen. Now, as he slid on his chest and belly to within inches from the track, he felt siezed with near panic. The iron wheels were so close he could feel grit and sparks, and the railroad ties under his body shivered as each heavy wheel passed.

Clint crabbed back away from sure death and came to his feet just as the caboose loomed into view. The footing was bad and the Gunsmith could feel wetness in the palms of his hands where gravel and cinders had torn his flesh. He planted his feet and as the caboose shot past, Clint threw himself at the handrail that ringed the rear platform.

He felt a tremendous jolt through his arms and shoulders and then his body was catapulted skyward. Smashing into the rail, his grip was almost torn away.

The conductor riding in the caboose jumped out on the rear platform and shouted, "Let go, you fool!"

Clint's legs were dangling and his boots were taking a hell of a pounding as they were dragged over the railroad ties.

"Let go, I say!"

The conductor had a little baton and he rapped Clint across the knuckles. But the Gunsmith was already in so much pain he didn't feel a thing. "Help!" he shouted in anger. "Goddamn you, give me a hand up!"

"No!" the conductor rapped him again, and Clint cussed a blue streak. When the man siezed his thumb and began to pry it back, Clint took a desperate gamble. Releasing one hand, he threw his arm out and grabbed the conductor by his shirt front and then yanked him completely over the rail.

The man's scream ended very abruptly, but Clint did not have time to see him strike the railroad bed and then lay groaning with a broken arm. The Gunsmith was much too busy hauling his own battered carcass over the rail before he collapsed on the rear platform of the caboose and lay gasping for air.

"Son of a bitch!" he wheezed. "How come nothing ever comes easy!"

EIGHTEEN

Miranda's father knew something was amiss when he heard the great bell in the steeple of St. Mary's begin to toll late that evening. He listened to the bell and chewed at his fingernails and then he threw his dime novel to the couch and began to pace the floor.

But after ten minutes of pacing, and even after the bell had stopped tolling, he was still too agitated to sit down. It had been hours since Miranda had left to visit the jail and see Clint Adams and still had not returned. What could have gone so wrong and why had the damned church bell been ringing so loudly?

The more he thought about it, the more Hale knew that he had to investigate. Miranda might be in serious trouble, though he was not exactly sure what kind of trouble.

The ex-sheriff pulled on his coat and slipped a gun into his pocket. He had a vague, uneasy feeling that his own life was in danger. Mostly, that feeling was based on the fact that he knew too much about Rick Hadley and had always figured his safe edge to be that the man would not kill the father of his fiancée. Now, that edge was missing and Hale knew that Rick would be incensed when he learned that Miranda had gone to visit the Gunsmith.

Virginia City was all astir as people rushed down toward the Catholic church to see what all the fuss

was about. By the time that Hale arrived, the priest
had already explained over and over that there had
been a mistake.

"How the hell can anyone pull a bell by mistake!" an angry listener demanded.

Fr. Doolin smiled benignly. "No one is perfect,
my son. Even so, that is no excuse, and I sincerely
apologize for creating such an alarm."

The crowd grumbled, but there was little they
could say now that the damage was done—the few
children who lived on the Comstock were awakened,
and everyone had interrupted their carousing to come
on down and find out what was happening.

The ex-sheriff started to turn around and go back
home but froze in his tracks when someone recognized him and said, "I'll bet your daughter will never
show her face on the Comstock Lode again!"

The sheriff blinked. "What do you mean?"

"You know damn good and well what I mean."

"No, I don't. But you'd better get right to explaining it to me!"

"Easy, Hale. You ain't the sheriff any more. You
got no badge to hide behind."

Hale felt himself tremble. "I want to know what
you're talking about! Where is my daughter!"

"She's gone away with the Gunsmith, you fool."

Another miner chimed in. "He knows that!"

Hale's composure broke. He grabbed a miner by
the neck and shook him hard. He was surprised by
his own strength. "Now tell me, damn you!"

The other miners pulled them apart. The one he'd
nearly choked wanted to fight, but he was held by
his friends, one of them who said, "Just in case you
really don't know, your daughter—along with Honey
Day—are the cause of all this trouble with the Gunsmith getting loose. And I'll just bet that this church
steeple business was tied to it in some way."

Hale took a backstep. "Wait a minute! Are you trying to tell me that my daughter and that saloon girl helped the Gunsmith escape!"

"They sure as hell did!" a burly miner growled. "Along with that skinny drunk named Boswell. He tricked the whole bunch of us by makin' up the Gunsmith to look like a woman! A purty one too!"

The sheriff blinked. "Did they kill Max Bullock?"

"Nope, but he's still stretched out colder than a Tahoe trout."

Hale swallowed nervously. "I . . . I can't believe this," he mumbled.

"You better watch out for yourself!" a man said, shoving Hale roughly. "The way we see it, your daughter tricked all of us and she's gonna pay!"

Hale wanted to pull his gun and shoot the belligerent son of a bitch, but instead, he hurried away, his mind in a high state of agitation. In fact, he was so agitated that he did not see Rick's two saloon bouncers who came up behind him and shoved their guns in his spine.

"Just keep on moving," one said in a hard voice as he searched Hale and then removed his six-gun. "But turn on "D" Street and keep walking south."

"Where to?"

"You'll find out when we get there."

Hale felt his guts churn with fear. "Listen, boys," he said. "When you see Mr. Hadley, I want you to tell him that I tried to talk my daughter out of getting involved with the Gunsmith. I begged her to listen to reason, but you know how strong a young woman can be."

"Shut up," one of them growled, jamming his gun deep into flesh. "You can tell Mr. Hadley all about it yourself."

"He's going to be out here?" Miranda's father could not believe this was happening to him.

"That's right."

"Well," Hale said, trying to put some bluster into his voice. "I'm not too damned happy about having a gun shoved into my spine and then marched out of town. I'm gonna tell Mr. Hadley about it too. I'm sorry about the Gunsmith getting . . . uhhh!"

Hale doubled up with pain when a fist smashed into his right kidney. He would have buckled to his knees if one of them hadn't grabbed him by the coat and hauled him up on his toes.

"We already told you to shut up, you fat, mouthy bastard."

Hale drew in a sharp breath. The punch had brought him more pain than he'd had to suffer in years. Maybe in his youth he could have figured out a way to fight back, but not anymore. Never had he felt so helpless and hopeless.

Still, as they walked out of town, his anxiety increased with each step until he knew he had to risk speaking again. "Listen, just tell me this much. Is Mr. Hadley angry with me? Surely he doesn't blame me for what my daughter did!"

"One more word and I'll save Mr. Hadley the trouble and kill you myself."

Hale knew he was as good as a dead man. Rick was going to kill him, and he was going to do it somewhere out here in the brush, then probably throw his body down an abandoned mine shaft and cover it up or else bury him under a pile of tailings. Either way, he was a goner, and it was likely that his body would never be found.

As they left Virginia City farther and farther behind, Hale felt an overpowering sense of despair. But then, he began to dredge up some courage and think about ways he might escape. Sure, there probably wasn't any, but at least he would die with some dignity. He resolved not to whine or beg for his life like some coward. He'd been a sheriff for too many years to crawl during the last few minutes of his life. It was all right to be cunning, if he could save his life, but he'd not beg and plead like he'd seen other men do when it came time to cash in their chips.

"Move around that big tailings pile," one of the bouncers ordered. "Just don't try and run. You're too fat and big a target to miss."

"You wouldn't dare fire a shot that would be heard."

"I meant miss with my knife," the man said. "I'd sink my blade through your other kidney. You'd die the worst death you can imagine."

Hale had seen a lot of death, and his imagination was plenty vivid. So he kept quiet, and when he skirted the tailings pile he was pale and grimacing.

"Take it easy," Rick said brightly. "You look as if you were about to be hung."

The sheriff said, "Hung, shot, stabbed, or garroted, what's the difference."

Rick frowned. "What the hell are you talking about? No one is going to hurt you. I just want to talk."

Hale did not believe Rick. "Talk about what? About my daughter?"

"Sure, that's a good start. Where did she and Honey take the Gunsmith to hide?"

Hale shrugged his round shoulders. "I don't know. I didn't even know that she was planning to help him escape. Last time I saw her, she said she was just going to talk to him."

"Why?"

"I have no idea."

Rick's smile faded in the moonlight. "That's not nearly good enough," he said. "You'll have to do better."

"I can't. It's the God's honest truth, Mr. Hadley. I didn't know she was going to be stupid enough to help him escape. I didn't think it was even possible with an entire lynch mob out front and no back door."

"Where would she take him?" Rick asked, his voice smooth and easy.

"I don't—"

Hale did not finish. With a twisted grin on his face, one of the two big men reared back his fist and smashed him in the mouth. Hale found himself sitting on his butt with stars flashing behind his eyes and broken teeth scattered across his tongue. He swallowed some of them along with his own blood and tried to clear his vision.

"Get him up," Rick hissed.

"Once more, where is the Gunsmith and your two-faced bitch of a daughter?"

Hale shook his head until he could see Rick's face swimming before him. He knew he was a dead man and that there was nothing left to lose. Dimly, it occurred to him that if he was going to die he'd rather it happened in a hurry. So he did what he figured would earn him a quick, merciful bullet. He spat blood and a few pieces of his own teeth straight into Rick's handsome face.

Rick went crazy. "Goddamn you!" he screeched, rearing back his own fist and driving a right cross into the sheriff's nose that broke it like a squished mellon.

The sheriff's mind went blank, just as he had intended it should.

"You know where to dump him," Rick said to his two men.

They both nodded. "Same place Dave Fartley is restin'," he said, "though I imagine poor old Dave is nothing but bones by now."

Rick watched them drag the sheriff over to the shaft, his bootheels raising little clouds of dust. He picked up a rock and tossed it into the hole, and he counted to six before it struck the bottom, far, far below. All three of them heard the ominous rattling of snakes. "It's got to be at least two hundred feet deep," he said. "Maybe as much as three."

The two bouncers leaned out a little over the shaft which was about ten feet across and had boarded sides. "Whatever it is, I'll bet them rattlers are bitin' that poor bastard like crazy. Fillin' him with all kinds of poison," one opined.

Rick shivered a little. "I was thinking about this shaft one night when I was screwin' Honey. I was thinking about how it would be the worst kind of torture to tie a rope around a man and lower him to dangle within a few feet of the snakes. He'd go out of his mind with fear. One thing sure, if we'd have done it to Hale, there's no doubt he'd have talked a blue streak."

One of the bouncers said, "Only problem is, Hale was so fat that it would have taken at least five of us to lower him down and then another bunch to drag him back up once he talked."

"Who said anything about dragging him back up just because he talked?"

The two powerful bouncers exchanged worried glances. Rick Hadley wasn't kidding and, once again, it occurred to them that he was not a man to be crossed.

NINETEEN

Clint walked through the caboose and stepped out to the front platform. He climbed an iron ladder and jumped into the next forward car which was filled with ore. Wading through the loose rock, he made his way forward on the train jumping from one car to the other until he came to the flatcar where Miranda, Honey and good old Boswell were sitting. Boswell had managed to somehow procure a fifth of whiskey and the three were celebrating their escape from the Virginia City lynch mob.

"Come on down and join us!" Miranda called.

Clint was plenty happy to do that. He climbed down the ladder and walked across the flatcar, then took a seat beside them. Boswell handed him the whiskey saying, "I'm afraid these ladies have drank almost all of it."

"I'll bet," Clint said, taking a long pull on the bottle and feeling the fire of the liquor flow right down to the bottom of his gut where it banked as hot as the coals in a pot bellied stove.

The Gunsmith handed the bottle back to the actor and stretched out on the hard, wooden floor of the car. Propping his head up on one arm, he watched the dark landscape sweep past as the train cork-screwed its way down from the Comstock. It was a steep grade and brakes were smoking by the time they reached the flat desert floor and then rolled east toward Carson City and its huge roundhouse station where the trains were unloaded, repaired and boarded.

The clackety-clack of the rails was so loud that conversation would have been difficult, so the four of them did not even attempt to discuss their next move until the train stopped and they hopped off.

Carson City was quiet and its residential streets were dark as they walked into town in search of a saloon or hotel where they might get something to eat and sleep at this late hour.

"We're leaving on the first train east," Boswell said. "It's New York for us."

"Do you have the money for a ticket?" Clint asked.

"I do, thanks to Miss Day's generosity." He reached into his coat pocket and held up the broach that Miranda had been forced to offer him in exchange for his assistance in helping to free the Gunsmith. Boswell admired the jewelry in the light of the moon. "This magnificent broach that Miss Hale so kindly bestowed upon me will bring a pretty price in Reno."

Clint snatched the broach from the man's bony fingers. "It still belongs to her," he said.

Boswell was furious. "Sir, these ladies and I had a deal!"

Clint was just as angry as he gave the broach back to Miranda. "I don't know what kind of a deal you made to help them, but I'll tell you this, in exchange, I'll write and sign a short account of what we have been through on the Comstock. You'll need some kind of proof or nobody will believe what really happened."

Boswell rubbed his chin. "What about that which remains to happen? I have a feeling that this story is not over."

"It isn't," Clint said. "I'll be taking a train right back up to the Comstock once I'm sure that you are all safe and out of Rick Hadley's grasp."

"Then that's the story that will sell," the actor said. "I need to know the ending."

"Is it worth risking your lives to remain here in Carson City?"

Boswell considered that a moment before he nodded. "I think it is. I can wire a few of my old friends who can contact a New York publishing house which will pay me handsomely for the account. I can also be working on a screenplay for the Broadway stage. Of course, you must promise me, Mr. Gunsmith, that this tale will have a satisfactory conclusion."

"I wish I could make that promise," Clint said as they entered the main street of the territorial capital. "But I'm afraid the conclusion is still very much in doubt. I know that Rick has gone bad, and I suspect he had his partner, Dave Fartley, murdered. But so far, I have no proof of anything, and I'm a hunted man up there. Obviously, I've got my work cut out for me on the Comstock."

"And my father," Miranda said. "Will you make him leave at once?"

"I'll strongly encourage him to come down here at least until Rick Hadley is behind bars," Clint said.

Honey had been listening to all this. "Rick is no good," she said. "Just don't trust him for a minute."

"I don't," Clint added. "Not anymore. I'm sure that he's the one that was behind that lynch mob and supplied the whiskey and beer. He was out to finish me off, and there will be no quarter asked or given between us."

"There's the Ormsby House Hotel," Miranda said. "I'm sure that they will be able to put us up for the night."

"Good," Clint said, leading the way. "It's been a long, long day and night. I plan to sleep until noon and enjoy the tomorrow that I was afraid I might never see."

They had to awaken the night clerk who informed them that there was just one room available. "Are you sure that's the best you can do for us?" Clint asked.

"At this hour of the night, you ought to be grateful," the man said, knuckling the sleep out of his eyes.

"Then I guess we'll have to double up and take it," Clint said. "What about a bath?"

"You must be out of your mind if you think I'm going to heat water at two o'clock in the morning," the clerk snapped.

Clint was in no mood for surliness, but the man did have a point so he let it ride. "Give us our key."

"Cash for the room in advance," the clerk said. "No cash, no room."

Clint had had enough. He grabbed the clerk by the collar and yanked him up on his toes. "The key, and be damned quick about it!"

It was amazing how fast a sleepy desk clerk could become fully awake when supplied by the proper motivation. In an instant, the key was in the Gunsmith's hand. They trooped up the stairs, found their room and opened the door to see just one bed.

"Looks like you and me sleep on the floor, Boswell."

The old man groaned. "My bones are brittle and I'll barely be able to walk in the morning," he complained.

Miranda took pity on the man. "You can sleep with Honey, I'll take the floor with Clint."

"Are you sure, my dear?"

Miranda nodded. "I'm sure."

In less than five minutes, they had made their sleeping arrangements and were turning off the lights. Clint and Miranda had taken a pair of blankets and spread them out on the floor. It was still rock hard, but it would have to do. Honey climbed into the bed, and Boswell went right in after her, his eyes round with excitement. But when Clint blew out the light, Honey said, ''You keep your hands to yourself tonight, you old lecher!''

Her order was followed a split second later by the sound of her hand striking his face.

Clint grinned up at the darkness. Boswell was not going to have any fun this night. He'd managed to wheedle and con his way into the bed, but sleep was all he'd get for his trouble.

Beside him, Miranda lay wide awake and when Clint rolled over on his side toward her, he discovered that she was so close that he could feel the sweet warmth of her breath on his face.

Clint could not help himself. He reached out and pulled the young woman to his side, remembering her kiss and then reliving it as their lips met. Because they did not want to disturb either Honey or Boswell, neither Clint nor Miranda said a word as they slipped out of their clothes and embraced with a quiet yet very urgent passion.

Clint reached down and his fingers found, then explored Miranda's womanhood. He discovered, to his relief, that she was not a virgin, but when the Gunsmith mounted her, Miranda stifled a gasp for she was very tight inside.

Slowly and with great care, Clint's hips began to rotate in union with her own. Miranda's fingernails dug into his back deeper and deeper as her body began to surge up to engulf every bit of his throbbing manhood. A warm breeze played with the curtains and brushed across them as Miranda struggled to keep from crying out with pleasure.

Clint was in no hurry. He had a young woman who was not experienced in the art of lovemaking, and it gave him a good deal of satisfaction to know that Rick Hadley had obviously been denied. What experience she had was that of a woman who might have lost her senses for a brief, passionate encounter during her early teenage years.

Miranda was quietly coming apart as he drove her through one threshold of pleasure into another, each higher, each more exquisite until her head began to rock back and forth and her body was behaving as if it were independent of her mind. Dimly, she was aware that she could not cry out and that she should not be gasping so loudly, but she could not help it. And when she finally experienced the wonderful joy of a new fulfillment, she would have cried out involuntarily except that the Gunsmith's mouth closed over her own.

Miranda's body convulsed powerfully, and the Gunsmith, satisfied that he had brought her to her first climax, took the young woman in a frenzied rush, filling her with his hot seed until they both shuddered and were still.

Clint tasted the salt of tears on Miranda's cheeks. Had he hurt her after all? He started to climb off her, but when she wrapped her arms and legs tightly around him, he guessed he had better not move and that the tears were not from pain, but from joy.

That made him feel very, very good. Now, if he could save her father and bring justice to the Comstock, this entire affair really would have Boswell's "satisfactory conclusion."

TWENTY

The next day, Clint stopped a miner out on the street and said, "You and I are about the same size, how would you like to swap clothes?"

The man blinked, then surveyed the Gunsmith suspiciously. "Are you pullin' my leg? You're wearing thirty dollar boots, and that's a nice shirt. Those Stetsons don't come cheap either."

"That's right," Clint said. "And your clodhopper work boots are shot, your pants have holes in the knees and that old woolen shirt isn't worth more than two bits."

The miner grinned crookedly, "If what I'm wearin' is so bad and what you're wearin' is so good, what the hell do you want to swap with me for?"

Clint had to smile. "Because, Mister, you look like every miner I ever seen, right down to your suspenders, and I need a drastic change of appearance."

"You are serious," the miner said. "And I'm not a man to look a gift horse in the mouth. This cap of mine is a sorry thing, and my underwear are—"

"Never mind the underwear. I'm not swapping those. Just the cap, that old bandana, your shirt, pants and work boots."

"This must be my lucky day," the miner said, as Clint led off down the street until he came to an alley and ducked behind a rain barrel.

The trade took only a few minutes and Clint watched the miner saunter out into the street. His boots had fit a little tight, but the fellow had solved that by throwing away his filthy old socks. He stopped on the main street, waved good-bye to the Gunsmith, then strolled up the boardwalk looking as happy as could be.

Clint's mood was quite the opposite. He'd never been a fancy dresser, but he'd never looked this bad, either. The clothes he now wore were ill-fitting and dirty. The boots were a little too large, and it felt as if he had stepped into tubs of cement. When he came out on the boardwalk and then viewed himself in a storefront window, his mood darkened even more.

"They'll never recognize me in these rags," he said, consoling himself. "All I need to do is rub a little grime on my hands and face and I could walk right by Rick Hadley."

When Clint went to say good-bye to Miranda, she too was shocked, but then said, "It's perfect. If you smear a little dirt on your face and hands—"

"I already thought of that," Clint said without much enthusiasm. "Now, all I got to do is to find a way back up to the Comstock."

Boswell overheard him. "I think I already have a solution," he said.

Clint watched as the man strolled over to a freighter who was loading up supplies for the Comstock. Boswell pointed at Clint and the man shook his head. Boswell kept talking, and then he slipped the freighter a coin.

The freighter looked at Clint, then reluctantly nodded.

"It's settled," the actor said, returning to Clint's side. "That gentleman has agreed, for a very small renumeration, to give you a ride back up to Virginia City.''

''Thanks,'' Clint said. ''It's perfect.''

He turned and then kissed Miranda good-bye. ''I'll be fine and so will your father. Getting him off the Comstock will be my first order of business. Getting Rick Hadley behind bars will be my second.''

Miranda nodded and, behind her, so did both Honey and Boswell. They all looked very worried, perhaps Boswell as much as the women because, if the Gunsmith were to fail, it would certainly put a cold wash on his plans for a successful stage play.

Clint stepped over to a freight wagon and climbed aboard. ''I'm ready,'' he told the driver, a man he'd agreed to pay a couple of extra dollars so that he might ride along with him on his journey back up to Virginia City.

In answer, the driver cracked his whip, the eight-mule team leaned into their harness and the wagon was on its way.

They paralleled the Carson River east and then swung north and started climbing up the low, base mountains until they came to a point where the grade grew very steep. The teamster was not an especially talkative or friendly man and that was fine with Clint because he was not interested in idle conversation. He was still not sure how he was going to operate on the Comstock without someone recognizing him, and yet, he knew he had no choice but to boldly go forward and try to ferret out some piece of evidence against Rick.

Clint sat quietly as they passed through Silver City and then Gold Hill. When the wagon began the very steep climb up and over the divide into Virginia City, he said, ''This is far enough for me.''

''Jump then,'' the freighter said. ''I sure don't

want to stop dead on this grade. The mules would have a hell of a time getting us started again.''

Clint looked for a good landing place, and then he jumped off the wagon and landed solidly on his feet. Without a backward glance, he headed across the sagebrush intending to come into Virginia City from down near the V. & T. train depot.

It was just about sundown and he figured the first place he'd go would be to the Hale house and see if he could get the ex-sheriff to help do some snooping around. Hell, maybe the man would even cooperate enough to finger Hadley if the Gunsmith would guarantee his personal protection. If that were the case, then they could ride the ten o'clock train down to Carson City and find a judge in the morning. Arrest warrants could be issued, and then the Gunsmith was on solid, legal territory. He could make a citizen's arrest, and if Rick or one of his gorillas tried to stop him, he'd be within his rights to shoot them down.

As Clint walked along, he heard a dog's frantic barking. He saw the animal about a hundred yards away and he stopped, thinking it peculiar that the dog was so upset because there was nothing visible that would cause it so much agitation.

He angled over to the dog and when he got closer, he saw a pair of boot heel furrows and they led right over to an abandoned mine shaft. When the dog saw him approach, it wagged its tail.

"What'd you lose down there," Clint asked, studying the footprints on the ground.

"Help," came a faint voice from down below. "Help me, please!"

Clint forgot all about the dog. He came to the edge of the hole and peered down inside, but all was darkness. "Hey, down there!" he yelled.

"Help me," repeated the familiar voice.

"Hale, is that you?"

There was a long pause and then Hale said, "Clint?"

"Yeah, how far down are you!"

"I don't know," Hale said in a broken voice. "I think I'm a long way down. I . . . I just woke up a little while ago and I'm caught by my belt on a spike or something sticking out from the wall."

There was a long pause before the man added, "Clint, if my belt breaks, I'm a dead man. There are snakes down at the bottom! I can hear them!"

Clint swore softly. "Who did this?"

"Rick Hadley and his two henchmen, goddammit! Can we go over the details later!"

"Sure," the Gunsmith said, "just as long as we agree that you are going to swear to this and anything else you can think of when I get you safely down to Virginia City."

"All right! Just get me out of here and I'll do anything!"

Clint nodded. "You're going to have to hang on until I can get a horse and a lot of rope. It will take me an hour."

"Jeezus man! Get some help and—"

"If I do that," Clint said, "either someone will recognize me, or Rick will hear of the rescue, and you'll be in deep trouble again. I've got to get you out of here alone. You have to hang on."

"All right, just hurry, please!"

"I'll be back," Clint promised.

Because he did not want anyone else to be attracted by the little dog, the Gunsmith picked the mutt up and carried him into town, scratching his ears and making such a fuss over him that the dog would not stop licking his hand. When Clint reached the livery where he had boarded his black gelding, he set the dog down and said, "Go find someone else to scratch your ears and make a fuss over you. I've got too much to do right now."

The dog wagged its tail, and then it turned and trotted down the street to see what it could find.

Clint moved inside the barn and left the door open so he could see his way along, and when he heard the very distinct and familiar nickering of Duke, his face creased in a broad smile.

"Well," he said, finding his halter, blankets and bridle in the same little cabinet where he'd been instructed to leave them. "Seeing you again sure picks up my spirits."

He saddled and bridled his horse quickly, then rummaged around in the barn until he had gathered up every foot of rope to be found. It seemed strange to poke his round-toed work boots through his stirrups, but he wasn't complaining as he swung into the saddle and rode out the back door, skirted the corrals and headed south. It took him less than ten miles to return to the mine shaft.

Clint dismounted. "I'm back," he said. "You still hangin' by your belt?"

"Yeah," Hale gasped. "But I'm gettin' weaker and weaker by the minute. I won't be much help. And I can't move or I might break away from this spike. You'll have to come down and help me."

Clint was afraid of that. The last thing in the world he wanted to do was to lower himself down into that pit and fumble around suspended a couple hundred feet over a den of snakes, but there was no choice. He understood that it was a near miracle that Hale had snagged up on the side of the shaft. Any movement at all could tear the belt away and send him spinning to a certain death.

The Gunsmith took the end of the rope and tied it

around his waist. He'd done some roping on Duke and the animal knew enough to take up slack. Clint tested Duke's memory by tugging on the rope. The gelding stiffened and its forelegs braced outward until Clint let up some slack, and then Duke retreated until the rope was taut again.

"Just do that when I need to come up again," he said as he edged over to the shaft, then slowly eased himself down the boarded side.

It was rough, dangerous and unpleasant. As it turned out, the real miracle was that Hale had not been ripped to shreds by the hundreds of spikes that protruded from the boarded up sides of the shaft. Clint had a hell of a time keeping himself from getting caught by the spikes and when he finally touched Hale with his boot, he guessed he had dropped at least a hundred feet.

"I can't see a damn thing down here!" he grunted.

"Give me the rope," Hale groaned. "This damn belt is about to cut me in half. It's agony."

"That damn belt saved your bacon," Clint reminded the man as he groped down to his side. "Now comes the tricky part."

Clint felt the sheriff reaching for the rope and he said, "Freeze, dammit! Don't do anything until I say so or we'll both feed those rattlers."

"Can you hear those dirty bastards?" Hale said. "I got a hunch that's where we'll find Dave Fartley's bones."

Clint grabbed a solid spike and found two more to stand on before he dared to untie the knot around his waist and grope for the sheriff. He found the man's belt and it was a good two inches wide and thick. "No wonder this didn't break," he said, tying the rope through the man's belt.

The sheriff grabbed the rope and clung to it tightly. "How many horses you got up on top?"

"Just one," Clint said, "but he's a hell of a stout animal and he can pull a little."

"I hope to hell you're kidding," Hale said. "I weigh two hundred and fifty pounds!"

Clint said, "Find a couple of spikes to put your weight on."

"Why?"

"Because my horse won't start pulling until I first give him some slack! Just do as I say and stop asking questions."

The toes of Hale's boots thudded against the wall for a minute until he apparently found two spikes to stand on. "Now what?" he grunted.

"Now lift yourself up off the spike that's caught in your belt, and we'll see if Duke can do what he's been trained to do."

"You mean you ain't sure he can!"

"No," Clint admitted. "But if he can't, I got the strength to pull myself up and out of here."

"Well where the hell does that leave me!"

"Right down there with the snakes," Clint said, his patience getting very thin, "now let's give my horse some slack."

The man did his best, and when Clint snapped the rope a few times, it began to inch them up the shaft. It was slow work, and both Clint and the sheriff had to keep stopping and getting themselves unhooked from the damned spikes that obstructed their ascent; but they got it done, and Duke performed like a champion.

When they finally neared the lip of the shaft, he could hear the big gelding puffing and stomping as he pulled ever farther back from the shaft, his shod hooves ripping sage in the darkness.

"There!" Clint said when he popped over onto solid ground, and then reached for Hale who was having an awful time and sounded to be in considerable pain. There was a moment when he was not sure he and Duke together could drag the fat man over the lip of the shaft, but they finally succeeded.

Clint wobbled to his feet. His clothes were badly torn and so was his flesh from the level of his chest right down to his boot tops. It was just as well that he'd traded clothes with the miner, his would have been ruined anyway.

Clint staggered out to Duke and took the gelding's bit. "Whoa there," he said, "easy now."

The big horse was trembling from exertion and even though the ordeal had lasted less than thirty minutes, the animal was drenched with sweat.

Clint untied the ropes from his saddle horn and wrapped his arms around the animal's neck. "Boy," he said, "are you worth your weight in gold dust."

Duke nickered softly in the night. He nuzzled Clint, plenty glad to be out of a stall and back with his master.

TWENTY-ONE

Clint and Hale returned to Gold Hill and, when they reached the ex-sheriff's house, Hale made them a pot of coffee and they sat on the back porch and discussed strategy.

"Rick Hadley has a monopoly on ruthlessness in this town," the sheriff began. "He pretty much takes what he wants and if anyone opposes him he has them shot or, like me, they just disappear."

"What kind of solid evidence can you give to put the man in prison?" Clint asked. "Since there were no witnesses tonight, it will be his word against yours when it comes to throwing you down a mine shaft."

"Dave Fartley's body is down at the bottom of that pit, I bet anything on that. There may be more."

"Still no evidence that he did or commissioned the murders," Clint said. "Hell, you were a sheriff for long enough to know that. What we need is some solid proof that he murdered Fartley and tried to murder you."

The fat man shrugged helplessly. "What you're asking is for something I don't have. Rick would never leave a shred of evidence against himself on paper. And those two goons he has doing his dirty work sure aren't going to talk."

"Then that leaves us right back where we started,"

Clint said. "We have exactly nothing to offer a court of law."

The Gunsmith stood up and frowned. "Rick was my blood brother, but he's gone as wrong as a lobo wolf. He's got to be stopped."

"I agree," Hale said. "But without evidence . . ."

Clint pulled his six-gun out from his baggy miner's pants. "Sometimes," he said quietly, "a man has to go outside of the law to do what the law intended."

Hale's eyes widened. "Meaning?"

"Meaning that the law intended to stop criminals and murderers like Rick Hadley, but it's hamstrung without solid evidence. We both know that Rick and those two men tried to kill you. They beat the hell out of you and tossed you down a mine shaft into a den of rattlesnakes."

"But you just said it would be my word against theirs!"

"That's right. So I'm going to have to take matters into my own hands and kill them."

Hale shook his head. "If you do that, you'll hang for certain. Rick is smart. He's given a lot of money to charities, and there are plenty of folks in this town who believe he's a fine and generous man."

"We don't and neither does Bill Meeker."

"You planning to ask him to help you?"

"Why not? I think we could use all the help we can get."

The sheriff was not enthusiastic. "Now, if you was talking about Jim Banks, I'd say you had something because he was a fighter. But Bill Meeker is another breed of cat."

"Will he fight?"

"Hell yes, but—"

"Then I'll ask for his help," Clint said. "Will *you* fight?"

Hale nodded. "I will."

"Then it's three against three," Clint said. "I consider even odds a luxury."

Hale studied Clint's face. "Let's get this done tonight," he said. "I want to either be a dead man come sunrise, or a man who can start to breathe easier knowing that he don't have to worry about getting ambushed anymore."

Clint tapped the barrel of his six-gun against the palm of his left hand. "That just suits me right down to the ground," he said. "Let's go to the Sawdust Saloon and get Meeker. Then we'll find Rick and settle this thing once and for all."

"I'll get my gun," the sheriff said quietly. "And tonight, for the first time in a long while, I reckon I'll have to use it."

The Sawdust Saloon was busy when Clint and Hale went inside. The Gunsmith, dressed as a miner, did not attract any attention except by a few who edged away because he was dressed so raggedly. Clint took a corner table and waited as Hale went and found Meeker and brought him over to talk.

"Hell, man!" the saloon owner said. "The whole town was hunting for you last night! Nobody's going to recognize you in those rags."

"That's the idea," Clint said, his voice low. "Sit down and let's talk a minute about Rick Hadley."

At the mention of Hadley, Meeker's face stiffened. "He ambushed my partner, Jim Banks, and he'll do the same to me one of these days."

"That's right," Clint said. "So what we have to do is to brace him and his men on our terms, not his.

I figure that you, me and Hale ought to be able to handle Rick and his two hired guns and muscles.''

"He's got a lot more help than that," Meeker said.

"Yeah, but those are the only two that are always around him," Clint said.

Meeker expelled a deep breath. "I just don't know."

"What don't you know? He killed your partner and he's going to kill you one of these days. What could be plainer?"

"You're right," Meeker said. "I have to act now or I'm a walking dead man. Do you have a plan?"

Clint thought about it for a moment before he answered. "The only thing I can think of is that we lure him and his men out somewheres, and then we settle this thing once and for all.''

"When?"

"Tonight," Clint said.

Meeker nodded stiffly. "All right. Tell me what I can do."

"You got a piece of paper and a pencil?"

"Not on me, but I can get one."

"Do that," the Gunsmith said, "and while you're at it, bring us a couple of beers."

"On the house," Meeker said, as he hurried back to the bar.

He returned with a pitcher of beer and said apologetically. "It ain't as good as the brew that Rick Hadley makes, but it ain't bad. I've been trying to figure out for years how Rick makes such good beer."

"It's the water he uses," Clint said. "He gets it in kegs from Lake Tahoe and sneaks it into his brewery at night."

"Well I'll be goddamned!" Meeker said. "Why didn't I think of that?"

Clint shrugged. "Give me the paper and pencil. I have a note to write."

When Clint had his writing materials, he frowned and printed just one short line. I'M NOT DEAD YET. SEE YOU TONIGHT AT THE V. & T. DEPOT. YOUR BLOOD BROTHER.

The other two men stared at it for a moment and then Meeker said, "Will that do it?"

"It will," Clint said. "I know Rick Hadley. He likes to gather up loose ends just like I do. He'll come, but he won't be alone."

Hale nodded. "Besides the pair of thugs he's always got nearby, he might bring another gunman or two."

"We'll be ready," Clint said. "We may be out-gunned, but we won't be outshot."

Hale and Meeker nodded. Both men knew that their backs were against the wall in this, and there was no way out short of running away and never coming back. Meeker had a saloon and he would not leave. Hale . . . well, he hadn't done much up until now, but Clint had a hunch that this time, the man really was ready to fight.

TWENTY-TWO

It was long after midnight and the Gunsmith was all alone on the boarding platform of the deserted V. & T. Railroad depot. He sat propped back in a wooden chair and watched the dark hills and the lights of Virginia City.

Three empty railroad cars waited to be used the following morning and in two of them waited Bill Meeker and the ex-sheriff of Gold Hill with their guns ready.

Clint looked up at the night stars and thought about his life and how he and Rick Hadley had once spent a good part of a summer night trying to count all those stars, but then, they'd fallen asleep and lost track of everything.

The Gunsmith wondered what had gone wrong with Rick. He'd certainly been a good and generous kid when they'd grown up together. But somewhere along the way, Rick had taken a wrong path in life and wound up twisted and ruthless. It was a tragedy.

"Here they come!" hissed Meeker from the box-car where he lay in wait. "All three of them!"

Clint eased the front legs of his chair down to the platform. Almost languidly, he stood up and stretched, first his legs, then his upper body and finally the muscles of his arms and fingers. He was entirely relaxed and ready for a fight.

181

"Over here," he called, as Rick and his two big gunmen hesitated and stopped about fifty yards out from the lonely train station. "I'm waiting for you over here."

Rick spotted his dark silhouette and said, "Step out into the moonlight where we can see you, Clint. Don't hang back in the shadows."

Clint decided to oblige his old friend. He stepped out to the edge of the platform and said, "I was hoping you'd come alone, but I should have known you'd bring your trained monkeys to tag along beside you."

"You know I like the odds in my favor," Rick said. "I always did."

"Yeah, but when we were kids, you never stacked the deck," Clint said. "And I can see that your friends are holding shotguns. Don't seem quite fair to me."

Rick laughed softly. "Life is never fair," he said. "Too bad you couldn't learn that for yourself. And it's too bad you didn't stick with me like I wanted. I'd have made you a fairly wealthy man if you'd played by my rules."

"I never play by someone else's rules," Clint said. "And by the way, what did you do with Miranda's father?"

"Threw him down a mine shaft," Rick said matter-of-factly. "After you're dead, you'll be joining him, along with Dave Fartley and a couple of others. Nice thing about this particular mine shaft is that when anyone snoops around it and hears the rattlers down below it makes them clear out fast."

"How clever," the Gunsmith said.

Rick shifted his weight slightly to the left as his right hand inched a little closer to his gun. "Where is Miranda?"

"She's safe from you." Clint paused. "I'm glad that she was the one thing you haven't ruined up here on the Comstock."

Rick's face contorted with rage. "Hit him boys!"

Clint saw Rick and the other two make their play, but he did not see the pair of riflemen who had crawled through the sage and were almost in firing position when Rick jumped the gun and shouted his order. The riflemen both fired prematurely but even so, the Gunsmith felt the heat of their bullets pass his face. He stepped back into the shadows just as his six-gun cleared leather and came level.

His first shot hit Rick in the side and spun him completely around and his second bullet killed one of the shotgun men outright. But the other man with the shotgun did manage to squeeze off a blast and the edge of the pattern caught the Gunsmith in the left arm and knocked him into some packing crates. Clint picked himself up as Hale and Meeker opened fire from the boxcars. Clint slithered across the platform and as one of the hidden riflemen returned fire at Hale, the Gunsmith aimed at the muzzleflash and silenced the rifleman with three quick shots.

Bill Meeker killed the other shotgun man who was frantically trying to reload.

His left arm leaking blood, Clint walked quickly over to Rick and knelt at the man's side. Clint touched his cheek and said, "You never gave me a choice."

Rick's lips moved soundlessly and then, he shuddered and died.

"Hale bought it, too," Meeker called. "The rifleman shot him through the head."

"Damn," Clint whispered. "It'll go tough on Miranda when I tell her."

The gunsmith ripped off his shirt, and Meeker

bound it tightly around his left arm to stanch the
flow of blood. When he was finished, Clint walked
around to the other side of the depot where he'd tied
Duke to keep the gelding safe from any stray bullets.
He mounted and rode around to survey the bodies
and then, without a word, he started to rein his horse
south toward Carson City.

"Hey!" Meeker called, hurrying after him. "There's
gonna be a big mob down here any minute, what do
I tell them!"

"If you're smart, you'll hightail it into the brush
and on back to Gold Hill without telling anyone
anything."

Meeker's jaw dropped. "You mean just let them
find all these bodies without ever knowing who killed
them?"

"Does it matter?" the Gunsmith asked quietly.
"All that counts is that, except for Hale, they all
needed killing."

"But . . ."

Clint stared down at the man who was looking up
at him with confusion. "Listen, Bill, you just tell
'em whatever you want," he said, touching his spurs
to Duke's flanks and sending the gelding into a trot.

But after a moment of indecision, Bill Meeker
came running after him. "You had it right," he
said, jumping sagebrush and running as fast as his
short legs would carry him. "Hey, I don't suppose
that big horse of yours would ride double long enough
to take a little fella like me on back to Gold Hill."

Clint reined Duke up. He kicked his left work
boot out of his stirrup and lowered his hand. Meeker
could not have weighed more than a hundred and
fifty pounds, and when the Gunsmith took his hand
and hauled him up behind his cantle, Meeker said,
"I am much obliged, Gunsmith. But your arm is a

mess. I'm afraid, if we don't get it taken care of quick, you might bleed to death before you get to wherever you're going."

"I'll make it as far as I need to go," Clint said quietly, as Duke spread the distance between them and the train depot where six dead men lay waiting to be found. "I always have."

Watch for

THE STAGECOACH THIEVES

*ninety-fourth novel in the exciting
GUNSMITH series*

Coming in October!

J.R. ROBERTS
THE
GUNSMITH